CAPTAIN'S DUET

Safe
Haven

 Red Phoenix

Safe Haven
1st Book of Captain's Duet

Cover by Shanoff Designs
Formatted by BB Books
Phoenix symbol by Nicole Delfs

Dedication

Why Captain and Candy first?

These two started off as side characters who quickly became fan favorites. I wanted to give you the backstory behind both these extraordinary characters in a way I've never done before.

Thank you, Anthony!

This is the man with the vision. He suggested I continue the Brie world by writing about characters within it. This duet was born from our conversation last year.

As far as the book itself,

I dedicate Safe Haven to the real-life heroes who, like Captain, willingly sacrifice themselves to protect our great country.

I also dedicate this book to submissives like Candy.

Subs who, because of inexperience, find themselves in questionable situations. Always trust your instincts, educate and protect yourself – Be safe.

My dear fans, I hope you loved diving deeper into Captain and Candy's story as much as I did writing it. I can't wait for you to read the next one!

But I won't lie, I was intimidated at first.

I wanted to do Captain justice as a serviceman in the

U.S. Army. Although I buried myself in a ton of personal research concerning the military, I depended on and am extremely grateful for the help of generous people who offered their knowledge and experience:

Top Griz (who combed the entire story pointing out issues and offering solutions), Master Brian (who provided his personal experience with a live fire exercise), and Aaron & Jessica Precht who provided important background knowledge concerning the Army.

Big thanks go to my incredible editor, Karen, as well as my proofer Jennifer B, and betas Becki W, Marilyn C, and Kathy O. This is a better book because of your influence.

I want to also thank my kids, Jon and Jessica. Your creativity, hard work, and dedication toward marketing this book has been amazing. So proud to be your mama!

Special kudos to my friend and fan, Brenda H, who does a ton of work behind the scenes. Thank you, thank you, thank you! What would I do without you?

I also want to give a special shout out to Kennia L - I've loved the hours spent chit-chatting at the pier about each book as they released. Thanks for continually spreading the love of Brie far and wide.

Last, but not least, I want to thank MrRed.

He continues to be my greatest supporter, encourager, and the inspiration for all my work. The depth of my love for him only increases with time.

SIGN UP FOR MY NEWSLETTER HERE FOR THE LATEST RED PHOENIX UPDATES

SALES, GIVEAWAYS, NEW RELEASES, PREORDER LINKS, AND MORE!

SIGN UP HERE

REDPHOENIXAUTHOR.COM/NEWSLETTER-SIGNUP

CONTENTS

For Country

Charles Walker

My family has served in the military for generations.
It's in our blood—
This driving need to serve and protect.

1976

Unlike many of my classmates, I know exactly where I'm headed and watch the clock with impatience as it slowly counts down the final minutes of my last day as a senior at Riley High.

Ellen keeps looking back from her desk two rows up, giving me a flirtatious smile. She's a cute little thing, and I know she's had her sights set on me ever since her latest beau broke up with her, but I politely look the other way.

I don't want to start anything—not when I'm about to leave town.

When the bell finally rings, I bolt from my chair and race out to the hallway. I hear Will call out, "Hey,

Charlie, you going to Arnold's party tonight?"

I hesitate, staring at the double doors at the end of the hall—the doors that mark my freedom. Personally, I have zero interest in the drunken parties Arnold is famous for, and I suspect the cops will be called to break it up long before the night is over. I can't afford that kind of hassle right now.

Turning to face Will, I tell him with a smirk, "I don't have time to waste. This guy's headed to boot camp."

"What's the rush, man? You can die for your country any time—you should live a little first, don't you think?"

I snort. "I have no intentions of dying, numbskull. In fact, when I return home, I'll already be moving up the ranks, while Arnold is still flipping burgers at the drive-in. You wait and see."

"You always were a stick-in-the-mud," Will replies good-naturedly. "So, will I be seeing you this weekend at the lake then?"

"No," I answer, my tone suddenly serious. "I'll be on the bus tomorrow to start my first week of training."

Will raises his eyebrows in disbelief. "You're serious, man?"

"Never been more serious in my life."

"Wow…" He scratches his head, looking as if he doesn't quite believe what I'm saying. "Which branch?"

"Army."

He laughs. "Now I know you're pulling my leg."

I grit my teeth, having had a similar reaction from my father. "You got something to say, Will?"

"It's just that everyone knows the Army is…"

"What?" I demand, my anger beginning to boil to the

surface.

I can tell he isn't looking for a fight, and he answers meekly, "…cannon fodder." He places his hand on my shoulder. "I just don't want to lose you, man. They got any desk jobs there in the Army?"

I shrug his hand off my shoulder. "You don't get it. I'm not joining the Army to sit behind a desk. I'm joining because I want to protect this country of ours."

"Then why not join the Air Force like your dad?"

"Not interested. I'm set on field artillery. I aim to protect the brave souls on the front lines. They should only have the best of the best shielding them with firepower, don't you think?"

Will shakes his head. "You always were an odd duck, Charlie. While I respect your decision, I have one piece of advice for you."

I am leery of what that "pearl of wisdom" might be.

"Come back alive, man."

"That's the plan," I answer bluntly. Despite my father's disdain for the Army, I am determined to prove myself and make him proud.

"Good luck, man," Will claps me on the shoulder. "But I'm sure the hell glad it ain't me." He gives me a friendly nod before heading down the hallway to his locker.

I look back at the double doors and start to sprint, not caring what others think. With a burst of youthful exuberance, I erupt from the doors screaming at the top of my lungs, "Freedom!"

Destiny is calling, and this man can't wait to meet up with it.

For Love

Cleopatra Cox

I believe love is the answer…
And I have found that answer in Ethan Haynes.

2012

I watch the clock tick down the seconds, marking the end of my time here at Riley High. I look over at Ethan and smile shyly, knowing we are going to celebrate tonight by making love for the first time. I think it's funny how the girls in my class are all weepy, and some even take pictures with their fancy phones to mark our last few minutes as seniors. Personally, I can't wait to get out of this place.

You see, I've had a crush on Ethan ever since I was a freshman. It happened the day he threw his math book to a friend and I unknowingly walked between them and got smashed in the face.

Hot damn! When Ethan looked down at me with those baby blues framed with long eyelashes and asked if

I was okay in that deep voice, my brain stopped functioning. I could only stare at him like a little lost puppy.

Ethan thought he'd really hurt me and insisted on taking me to the nurse's office. It was totally embarrassing, but I loved every minute of it.

After that, we started hanging out together every day. But, to my utter horror and disappointment, Ethan moved away two months later. His parents had suddenly decided to split up, and his mother headed off to New York, dragging Ethan with her.

To say I was completely devastated is an understatement.

All through high school, I watched my girlfriends date while I was completely ignored by the boys. You see, my girlfriends started filling out with those round curves that men can't stop staring at. But me? My body looked exactly the same—no boobs or hips to speak of.

Because of that, I was forced to endure cruel nicknames like Bee Sting and Pancakes. Oh yes, the boys thought they were being so clever and I would laugh it off. But damn, it hurt like hell.

My mom liked to tell me that I took after the fairies of her Irish homeland because of my big, round eyes, tiny frame, and wispy hair—but I knew better. I was a freak of nature, and if something didn't change, I would remain dateless for the rest of my life.

Thankfully, Ethan returned my senior year. He had moved back in with his father to finish his last year of high school, and I was back on cloud nine.

Oh, Ethan…

He was taller and even more handsome than before.

Just looking at that boy does things to me!

So here I am, anxiously watching the clock, ready to escape the insanity called high school. As soon as the bell rings, I pop out of my chair and grab the hand he's holding out for me.

Together, we walk out to the hallway and head straight toward the double doors that mark my freedom from this place.

Oh Lord, my body is already tingling just thinking about what's going to happen tonight, and I bite my bottom lip in anticipation.

I look up into those baby blues as we walk through the doors together. I can't wait to feel Ethan's love inside me...

Cast Away

Charles Walker

"Take the Money and Run" is playing in my head as I race home from school. I burst into the house, slinging the backpack off my shoulder and handing it to my little brother.

"It's officially yours now, kid."

He clasps it to his chest, beaming up at me. "Thank you, Charlie."

"Think nothing of it, little man. May it serve you well next year."

Jacob frowns. "But I don't want you to go."

I hit him on the arm affectionately. "Hey, I've got a country to serve."

My mother comes down the stairs. Her eyes appear puffy and red. Has she been crying? I rush over and give her a hug, whispering in her ear, "You knew this day would come, Mama…"

"It's not that," she sobs.

I pull away and look at her in concern. "Tell me

what's happened."

When she gazes into my eyes, I can see something is seriously wrong.

"Your father is waiting for you in the study," she tells me.

My mother looks so distraught that I give her another hug. She holds me tight as if she doesn't want to let me go. Rather than fight it, I continue to hold her until she finally releases her embrace.

"I love you, Charles."

I laugh lightly, seeking to ease her obvious distress. "I love you, too, Mama."

She seems so sad that it rips at my heart and I assure her, "It'll be okay. Whatever it is. Let me go talk to him."

My mother shakes her head as she takes Jacob's hand and leads him up the stairs.

I stare at her, wondering what the hell has happened. As I am about to head to the study, my mother stops at the top of the stairs and calls down. "Charles, I will always be proud of you."

I chuckle nervously, her sudden declaration making no sense at the moment. "Thank you, Mama."

She lets out a sob and turns away, pulling Jacob with her. My younger brother is looking at me with a goofy smile, holding up my backpack as he is dragged away.

I face the door of the study with trepidation, but walk briskly to it, determined to handle whatever has my mother so upset.

I knock on the door and wait until my father barks, "Enter."

I open it and enter the room, centering myself six

inches from the front of the desk. "Reporting as ordered, sir."

"Shut the door," he orders from behind his large desk.

I do so immediately, having learned at an early age to follow his orders without question.

"At ease. Take a seat, Charles," he states in a formal tone, as if he is speaking to a stranger.

I sit down and face him, my father's oversized desk acting as a barrier to separate us. To me, it is a physical representation of the emotional distance between us.

"Why is Mama crying, sir?"

He stares at me with cool disdain as if I should already know the answer.

I stand up to assert myself. "I asked a question, sir."

"Sit down! You know perfectly well that her tears have everything to do with you."

I sit down slowly, ice settling in my veins. I now understand what this is about, and I already know it will not end well.

"This is your final chance to do the right thing, Charles. You will not be given another."

I can't believe he is still harping about my decision to join the Army instead of the Air Force. "I've done nothing wrong, sir."

"I disagree. You can either do it the right way, or you can enlist in the Army now and ruin any chances of success."

I growl under my breath. His open disdain for the Army has always been a point of contention between us. "It shouldn't matter which branch I serve in."

My father clenches his jaw. He has long held the expectation that I would be a fighter pilot like him—and his father before him. Ever since I was a child, my father has groomed me to follow in his footsteps. However, I have no interest in flying, and have always had my eyes set on the Army. Although we disagree, I am a man now and had assumed he would respect my decision.

"You are far too intelligent to waste your talents. We've spoken about this on numerous occasions. You've been accepted and *will* attend the United States Air Force Academy.

"No, sir."

"I will not have a son enlist in the Army," he states coldly.

I narrow my eyes, clearly detecting the threat behind his words, but wanting him to say it out loud. "What do you mean, sir?"

He growls, "If you get on that bus tomorrow, there be will no reason to ever come back."

"Why?"

"You will not be welcomed in this home."

I understand now the reason behind my mother's tears. "Are you seriously that narrow-minded, sir?"

"Charles, let me make this perfectly clear since you seem to be a dull boy. I will not tolerate you wasting your future. It would be a disgrace to this family, and makes my oldest son seem like a fool."

"I guess I'm a fool then, sir."

My father erupts from his chair and points toward the door, bellowing at the top of his lungs, "Out!"

I remain rooted to the chair, stunned that he wants

to disown me for this.

"I said get *out*!" He marches to the door and opens it violently, his face a brilliant red, the veins in his neck pulsing with rage.

I'm still in shock, but I stand to face him. "I want to serve our country like the Walkers have for generations—and you have the gall to disown me for it?"

"You have a choice, Charles. The Air Force Academy or the Army."

I stare at him in disbelief, but I have the same Walker-born stubbornness he has running through my veins. There is no other choice for me.

"I choose the Army, sir."

His lips curl into a snarl. "Never come back. I'll have you arrested for trespassing if you do."

I roar like an angry lion as I rush past him, running up the stairs to grab my things. I won't stay another minute under his roof. I rush wildly to pack my clothes, stuffing them in my duffle bag, needing to get out of here as fast as I can—but realize I still need to say goodbye to my mother and little brother.

As I leave the bedroom, I find my father standing in the hallway like a sentry. I look past him, stating, "I've got to say goodbye to the family."

"You have no family here," he declares in a cold voice.

"You won't even let me say goodbye to them?" I challenge, spitting on the floor in disgust.

He sucker-punches me with such force that I stumble from the impact, my head hitting the wall behind me. Before I can recover, he grabs me and shoves me down the stairs, causing me to tumble out of control to the bottom.

I hear my mother's scream as he barrels down the stairs and drags me out of the house, throwing my duffle at me before locking the door.

I hear the lock settle into place, and it acts as my father's final statement: I have been locked out of my own family—permanently.

I rub my jaw in a daze as I stand up, my body aching from my tumble down the stairs. I slowly pick up my bag and turn away from the house. The outburst has brought out the neighbors, all of whom stare silently as I walk away from my home and everything I have ever known.

I fight off the tears that threaten to fall, confident I am not making a mistake.

No, this has only made me more determined than ever to make the Walker clan proud.

Heading straight to the bus station, I curl up on one of the empty benches and use my jacket as a pillow.

I close my eyes, still reeling from the shock…

Swept Away

Cleopatra Cox

E than gives me a quick kiss before I get on the school bus to go home. "So, I'll drop my dad off at his night job and then swing by in the truck to pick you up around 6:30. That work for you?"

"Sounds wonderful," I assure him, blushing deeply. We're really going to do this!

I get on the bus and sit in the back, so I can stare out the window. I don't trust myself to talk to my girlfriends, certain they will be able to tell what I'm up to.

This is *our* secret—just Ethan's and mine.

When I finally arrive home, I see my dad has already beaten me. I know he's worried about my mom because she's been consumed by what he and I have nicknamed "the dark place". It happens at least twice a year—Mom retreats into herself and stays there for weeks on end.

When I open the front door, Dad calls out from the kitchen, "Welcome home, C, my little high school graduate!"

I smile, amused by the fact he's shortened the ridiculous name he saddled me with to just one letter. "I'm not a graduate yet, Dad. You know I've got to get through the whole pomp and circumstance thing this weekend. Or did you forget?"

"About that…" he says with a pained expression. "Your mom—"

"I know, Dad. It's okay."

My dad gives me a hug. "She'd be there if she could, C."

I glance at their closed bedroom door. I've been through this countless times, and I have learned over the years to take care of myself whenever she gets like this. "Don't worry about me."

"But I want to celebrate this momentous day, so I'm making your favorite tonight—my dad's famous lasagna." He leans down and whispers in my ear, "I've even bought some wine. I think we ought to toast an accomplishment as big as this."

I'm deeply touched that he's gone to all the trouble, but I can't afford to stuff myself before I see Ethan, and my dad would expect nothing less than me eating two helpings tonight. I feel badly when I tell him, "Dad, I love that you did this, but I'm headed out tonight to hang with one of my friends. Can we do it tomorrow?"

I see the hurt in his eyes, but he nods and smiles. "Not a problem. I'll go ahead and put it in the fridge after it cools. It always tastes better the second day, anyway."

"Perfect."

I glance at their bedroom door, knowing he likes it

whenever I tell Mom about my day. To ease the guilt I feel for leaving him alone tonight, I tell him, "I'm going to let Mom know I've successfully made it through my last day of high school."

The smile returns to his eyes. "She'll like that, C."

He's wrong.

She won't even know I'm there.

I hate when my mom gets like this, but I like seeing my dad happy, so I turn to face the door, a pit in my stomach growing as I walk toward it. My mom is normally a fun person to be around, but not when she gets like this…

Opening the door slowly, I peek into the darkened room and see the lump on the bed covered in blankets. "Hey, Mom."

I look back at my dad and he winks as I close the door behind me.

"So, today was my last day as a senior."

Silence.

I stand over the bed and look down at her. My mother's eyes are open, but you can tell her mind is somewhere else.

"I'm graduating this weekend. Grandma and Grandpa will be there…"

But you won't, I add to myself.

More silence follows.

I decide to throw caution to the wind, needing *some* kind of response from her. "So, to celebrate, I'm going to make love to Ethan tonight."

Absolutely nothing. Not even a blink.

"Do you hear me, Mom? I'm going to lose my virginity tonight."

She stares off into space, lost in that darkness none of us can penetrate.

"You know, you're supposed to be there for me in moments like this. At least tell me we have to use a condom or something."

She doesn't make any outward sign she's heard me.

I growl as I turn to leave, muttering under my breath, "I don't even know why I bother."

I leave her alone in the dark, disgusted with myself for even trying, but still smile at my dad, who looks at me with a hopeful expression.

"How is she?"

"Same."

"Well, at least she knows you care."

I feel tears prick my eyes. *If only she cared too.*

I shake off the sadness, not wanting anything to ruin my night ahead. "I'm headed upstairs to take a relaxing bath and get myself ready for tonight."

"Where are you headed off to?" my father asks.

I shrug, purposely keeping my answer vague. "Probably watch a movie."

"No wild parties tonight?" he prods. "You know all you have to do is call and I'll come get ya. No questions asked."

I walk over and hug him. "I appreciate that, Dad. But I don't see the point of hanging with a bunch of inebriated teenagers. They're dumb enough sober."

He rubs the top of my head. "You've always been an old soul, C."

"Probably because you cursed me with an old person's name." I smirk at him and crinkle my nose.

He chuckles. "I know you secretly love it."

"*Right…*what girl wouldn't want the name Cleopatra?"

I head up the stairs, laughing.

Now for a long relaxing bath. I take extra time shaving my legs and primping for Ethan. Although my breasts are tiny and I look like a boy, I am all woman inside—and I want him to see that tonight.

In preparation, I secretly bought a set of sexy lace underwear and matching padded bra for tonight. I slip them on and look at my reflection in the mirror.

I feel giddy as I stare at myself, imagining what Ethan will think when he looks at me. He's always said I have the perfect body and insists he likes women with smaller breasts, claiming, "There's no need for more than a mouthful…"

Curious, I caress my nipples through the thick material of my bra, wondering what it will feel like to have him suck them.

Just thinking about it makes me wet, so I reach down and sneak a hand under my panties, feeling the slickness. The idea that he will be making me a woman tonight gets me feeling all weak and trembly inside.

I have never wanted anything this much.

I take extra time with my makeup, wanting to accentuate my eyes and lips, my two best assets. For the final touch, I dress in a short skirt, knee-high socks, and a white button-up blouse, attempting to capture the whole schoolgirl look.

When I bounce down the stairs just fifteen minutes

before Ethan is supposed to arrive, my dad looks at me and smiles. "Well, now, don't you look cute?" His expression suddenly changes. "Wait. Is this friend of yours a guy?"

"He is, Dad, and you even know him. I'm going to hang with Ethan tonight."

"Didn't he move away?"

"He did, but he's back now. Don't you remember me telling you that?"

I can't tell you the number of times he's forgotten something I've said, but I know it's because he's constantly worrying about Mom.

He scratches his head, looking a little lost and embarrassed.

"It's okay, Dad. You've got a lot on your plate. Anyway…you liked him then, and you'll like him even more now."

"The boy doesn't own a motorcycle, does he?"

"As a matter of fact, he does but he's in the middle of restoring it." When I see the worried look on my father's face, I add, "It's old and doesn't even run, so you don't have to worry. Ethan's picking me up in his dad's old pickup truck. I couldn't be safer."

"Good," my dad replies, seemingly satisfied, but then he frowns at me in concern. "You haven't had anything to eat yet."

"Ethan plans on feeding me." I feel the heat rise to my cheeks when I suddenly imagine sucking Ethan's hard cock.

"See? You're getting flushed from not eating. Let me get you something—"

The doorbell interrupts our conversation and I jump and then giggle nervously as I look at the door.

This is it…

"At least the boy knows to come to the door to pick up his date," my dad mutters as he opens it.

I let out a dreamy sigh when I see Ethan. He has gone all out and is wearing dress pants, a dress white shirt, and a tie.

Oh man, he looks so hot!

My dad holds out his hand and gives Ethan a firm handshake before letting him inside. "I trust you'll feed my daughter and have her home at a reasonable hour?"

Ethan glances at me and smiles charmingly before answering him. "Yes, sir."

"Dad, don't you think you should say hello to Ethan first?" I tease.

When I look back at Ethan, I'm totally captivated by those gorgeous blue eyes—so much so, that my dad notices.

"So, Ethan, I'm expecting you to treat my little girl like a queen tonight. She is, after all, Cleopatra."

"Yes, sir."

Ethan chuckles softly as he looks at me tenderly. "Your daughter deserves no less."

I can't wait to be alone with him. Taking hold of Ethan's hand, I lead him to the front door as I call out behind me, "See you, Dad."

"Have her back before twelve," my dad insists.

I turn around and look at him as if he's crazy. "I'm not a kid anymore."

Nodding, he thinks about it for a moment before

amending his edict. "Fine, make it one."

I shake my head at him, but Ethan answers, "One it is, Mr. Cox."

Once the door shuts behind us, Ethan lifts me up and twirls me in the air. "Now I've got you all to myself…"

A Man

Charles Walker

I can't sleep. My father's actions replay in my head, and I spend the night tossing and turning on the uncomfortable wooden bench.

At around 11:00, a security guard walks by, smacking his nightstick in his palm for emphasis. "Get up. Vagrants aren't allowed here."

I sit up slowly. "Not a vagrant, sir. Just waiting for my bus."

"This isn't a hotel, boy," he snaps, not even bothering to look at it.

I stand up, combing my hair back with my fingers, trying to look more presentable. "I understand, but my father and I have had a parting of ways and I have no place to stay tonight."

"Running away?" he states sarcastically. I look at the badge on his shirt and address him by name.

"No, Officer Hall. I've enlisted in the Army and am headed to boot camp in the morning."

The man slides his nightstick back into the slot on his belt and holds out his hand to me. "Thank you."

I look at his hand before taking it, wary of his sudden change of heart, but then shake it as a gesture of good-will.

His handshake is equally firm. "We need more patriotic young men like you."

"Thank you, sir."

The man suddenly frowns. "Your father must be a fool."

"Stubborn is the word, sir," I correct him, not wanting to disrespect my father no matter how furious I am at him right now.

"If I didn't work the night shift, I'd offer you a place to sleep," he tells me with regret.

I gesture toward the bench. "This works fine—if it's all right with you, that is."

"Of course, son."

He gives me a wink as he pulls out his nightstick and starts whistling, swinging the club in time with his tune as he walks away.

I stretch as I stare back at the bench, not ready to lie back down on it. Instead, I head off into the night to take a lap around the parking lot under the flickering light of fluorescent bulbs. I need to release the tension fighting with my father has stirred in me.

Luckily, I've found a good jog has the ability to reset my thinking—which I desperately need of right now.

When I finally return to my bench, I find a bag of chips, a sandwich and a bottle of water sitting there. I look around, but don't see any signs of Officer Hall.

I actually tear up as I rip open the plastic wrap, my stomach growling as I take the first bite. I'm touched by the man's thoughtfulness.

After a good run and a meal, I'm finally able to close my eyes and catch a few hours of sleep, but the moment I hear the birds start chirping just before dawn, making further rest impossible.

My recruiter comes to meet me at the station just before my bus arrives. He hands over my paperwork and bus ticket. "Make me proud."

"I aim to, sir."

I'm far too anxious for my new life to begin and board the bus early, feeling zero hesitation as I climb onto it. To my surprise, I spot Officer Hall standing at attention as the bus heads out of the station. Our eyes meet briefly, and I give him a nod, grateful for his send-off.

After hours on the road and many stops, we pull into another bus station where I join a group of fellow recruits as we transfer to a military bus. I sit next to a scrawny kid with disheveled red hair. Rather than looking excited, his downcast eyes and the way he keeps scratching the back of his neck tells me he's nervous. I am curious to know why.

Holding my hand out to him, I introduce myself. "I'm Charles Walker, and you are…?"

"Billy," he answers, smiling awkwardly as he takes my hand.

"Billy what?"

"Jackson. Billy Jackson."

"Nice to meet you, Jackson," I reply, shaking his

hand enthusiastically.

His awkward smile returns before he glances out the window, scratching at the back of his neck again.

"So, what made you want to join the Army?"

He looks back at me with an embarrassed smile. "My stepfather made me join. Said it would make a man out of me."

"And my dad forbade me from joining." I add with a chuckle, "We're like opposite sides of a coin, Jackson. Must be fate we met up today."

I see him relax a little. "Yeah."

I cross my arms and smile, confident he and I will make it through training together. Boot camp is where they separate the men from the boys, and I can't wait to be tested.

When we finally arrive at the reception station, we are ordered to walk single file into a large hall where the flags of all fifty states line the room. Jackson and I sit down on benches and are given simple instructions like responding to orders with a respectful, "Yes, Drill Sergeant."

That won't be an issue for me. My father taught me well, growing up.

We are also told to make a quick call home and we're instructed to say three sentences only. I stand in line waiting for my turn, but I feel the nerves set in, wondering who will be answering the phone when I call. I hope it's Jacob, because I want him to know I'm okay. I can't imagine what the poor kid must be thinking right now.

I dial the number and listen as the phone rings several times before it picks up. I immediately begin my speech. "I have arrived. I am safe. I will call you when I can."

"Don't bother," I hear my father say before hanging up.

I put the receiver down and nod to the guy behind me. Although his words cut me like a knife, I'm not going to let him control me. The anger I feel toward him can't outshine the satisfaction of being here—*this* is where I belong.

That night, I lie in my bunk, along with more than thirty other men. I hear the sighs and grunts of other recruits who are restless and in shock, finding themselves in this foreign environment. For them, this place is stifling and unfamiliar but, for me, this is my emancipation, and I can't stop smiling in the dark when I imagine how hard my father must be fuming tonight.

The following day, I get my PTs, the classic gray Army shirt and black shorts that makes up our physical training uniforms. I have wanted to wear these since I was a boy. Putting them on, I feel more settled.

Every step I take in this process makes it more real to me.

The second day at the reception center, however, is far from challenging or exciting. It is a day of waiting—waiting for blood work, waiting for a hearing exam, waiting for a dental screening and, at the end I get my official Army haircut. I rub the top of my head after I get out of the chair, liking the short cut. It's simple and requires no care.

I see Jackson outside, looking a bit dazed, so I clap him on the back. "What's up?"

"It's like being put through a meat grinder."

"How so?"

"We all look the same now, like they're trying to erase who we are."

I shake my head, looking around at the other recruits with haircuts like ours. "I don't see it that way at all. They're walking us through a series of steps designed to bring us closer together as a unit. One for all, all for one."

He snorts. "You have a strange way of looking at things."

I raise an eyebrow. "You think I'm wrong?"

"I wouldn't go that far. But how you perceive all this," he says gesturing around, "is not how I perceive it."

I slap him on the back again. "When we graduate from training, let's have this talk again."

I look around me, knowing we are about to enter a period of conditioning that will make us stronger physically, as well as quick to follow orders. The military tears down the individual to build up a team that is efficient in battle—and will ultimately save lives.

Basic training, and all that it entails, is necessary if we are to survive on the battlefield.

Late in the day I finally get to my physical fitness test and pass easily, which moves me into another line where I'm issued a duffle bag with my combat uniform. I proudly sling it over my shoulder, ending the day waiting in the last line to have my picture taken in uniform. I'm handed my military ID—which makes it official.

Back at the barracks, Jackson stops by to tell me,

"Hey, I heard we're headed out tomorrow." I watch as he scratches his neck nervously.

I smile, grateful for the news. "Good. It'll be fun."

He frowns and turns to walk away. I can sense he's really struggling and I want to encourage him. "I can tell you what to expect, if you'd like."

Jackson turns back around and nods as he scratches his neck again.

"You'll get yelled at constantly and fail over and over again. Don't fight it. Just follow orders and answer with a 'Yes, Drill Sergeant.' They're going to test our patience, barking repetitive orders to see if we can follow basic instructions. It's like a game. You can handle that, can't you?"

"Sure…" he answers.

"Just remember not to stand out. Don't be first and don't be last. Whatever they ask, you just suck it up and do what they tell you without complaint. The purpose of basic training is to get us thinking and acting as one."

"It doesn't seem so bad, the way you explain it."

I laugh as his naiveté. "Oh, don't kid yourself. The next two months are going to be hell."

Jackson frowns, doubt returning to his eyes.

"But it's hell with a purpose," I tell him confidently. "If you keep that in mind, it'll make it easier when things get rough."

"How can you be sure?"

"It's only nine weeks. I could hold my breath for nine weeks if I had to."

"Maybe you can…" he replies.

I'm concerned he is already questioning if he'll make

it to the end of basic training, so I tell him, "No matter what, you *will* get through this, Jackson. They're not out to break you, even if it seems that way. The reason they push so hard is to show us what we are capable of."

A guy three bunks down starts clapping slowly with a sarcastic look on his face. "Nice pep talk there. Where you from, Planet Bullshit?"

I laugh off his comment, not wanting to start anything. Instead, I agree with him as I settle back, folding my arms behind my head. "Guess I've been reading too many Army brochures."

"Fucking dick," the guy grumbles, turning on his side.

Jackson looks at the prick and shrugs, giving me a half-smile before heading off to his own bunk. I sometimes forget that not everyone feels the way I do about being here.

They haven't spent their entire lives waiting for this day to arrive.

I opt out of calling home to let my family know we're being transferred to the training battalion. I will not give my father the satisfaction of hanging up on me again. Instead, I write my little brother a letter, trusting that my mom will make sure he reads it.

Dear Jacob,

I know things were pretty messed up when I left, but don't worry about me.

I'm okay. Great, in fact.

But now that you're second in command, I need to ask a favor, little man. Can you look after Mom? Pitch in when she needs help and give her an extra hug from me from time to time.

As for Father, he deserves your respect. He's done a good job preparing us for military life, and I'm grateful for his training despite the huge fight we had.

As far as that's concerned, I hope what you take away from it is how vitally important it is to be true to yourself, no matter what. I have no regrets and I know, someday, I will make Father proud.

In the end, this is your life, Jacob. You only get one chance, so make the most of it.

I'll keep this first letter short, but I wanted you to know your big brother is thinking of you as I head off to boot camp.

Love,
Charlie

I seal the letter and then settle back in my bunk. Even though I'm exhausted, I can't fall asleep and suffer another restless night. Visions of the fight with my father replay in my head. The ruthlessness of his actions and words eat at me.

What if I am never accepted back into the family because of this? I'm overcome with a sense of foreboding. No, blood is thicker than water. Someday he will welcome me back home with open arms. Until that time, my only job is to work my ass off to prove I was right.

At 0430 in the morning, I jump out of bed, grateful to start the day and be free of my thoughts. After a quick meal in the mess hall, I head to the buses.

A female Drill Sergeant orders us to get on the bus quickly and quietly. Some recruits are slow getting on the bus, while others take their time choosing seats. That results in a tongue-lashing, and all of us are ordered off the bus to try again. Three attempts later, amid a series of spirited corrections, we are finally able to run onto the bus and sit down in a quiet and orderly fashion exactly as she instructed.

As punishment for being slow learners, she makes us belt out "God Bless America" until our throats hurt.

You would think we'd learned our lesson as a group, but no. When we exit the bus too slowly, we are forced to do it again before being separated into squads.

The Drill Sergeant for my squad introduces himself in a calm, collected voice as Drill Sergeant Herbert Marshall, but we are only allowed to call him Drill Sergeant.

If anyone has illusions that he will be easier on us than the previous Drill Sergeant was because of his quiet demeanor, they are sorely mistaken.

Our Drill Sergeant is disgusted by our lack of hustle getting off the bus and yells at us, "Drop your bags and do twenty now." He orders us to get back on bus, this time, we must line up alphabetically once we exit.

We start muttering our last names to each other, shifting in line until we have it but, naturally, we fail to do so quickly enough and get to do another set of twenty.

Afterward, the Drill Sergeant walks down the line with a disgusted look on his face. He stares at each of us critically, giving special attention to certain individuals who catch his eye—starting with Jackson. Unfortunately, the kid is nervous and scratches the back of his neck as he stammers out an answer.

Jackson is ordered to run in place, so he can get his thoughts in order. I can tell by the kid's red cheeks that he is humiliated at being the first of the recruits to be called out by the Sergeant.

Although I've tried to go unnoticed, the Drill Sergeant confronts me as well. "Do you have a problem?"

I stare straight ahead and quickly answer, "No, Drill Sergeant."

"I think you do. Drop and give me twenty."

I do so immediately and without question.

I hear the prick from the night before snort beside me. It doesn't go unnoticed by the Drill Sergeant, and he walks over to him next. "Do you find something amusing?"

The prick immediately frowns and shakes his head. "No, sir."

"Sir? You dare to insult me by calling me *sir*?"

"I didn't mean to, Drill Sergeant," he answers.

The Drill Sergeant addresses the entire squad. "Recruit Bell's insult will cost you all. Everyone drop and give me twenty."

I've just finished my punishment, but immediately drop back down to do twenty more. This prick has not only gotten on the sergeant's shit list, but he isn't winning any friends in the process. Until he learns discipline, all of us will be made to suffer for it.

That evening, just before lights out, the prick punches me in the stomach as I try to walk past him to my bunk.

"What the fuck, BS?" he shouts at me. "Why the hell are you trying to get me in trouble?"

I ignore the pain, getting right up in his face. "That's not my name."

"It is now." He looks around our barracks with a smirk on his face. "Everyone, meet BS here, official bullshitter of the Army."

I hear people chuckle, but I'm not concerned because I know exactly how to handle this guy. "Hey, I've got a name for you."

"Go ahead and say it before I punch that smug look from your face."

I smile wider and simply say, "Grapes."

"Grapes? What kind of fucking name is that?"

"It stands for sour grapes, which you seem to be severely suffering from right now."

The whole room bursts out snickering at the ridiculous name.

If looks could kill, I would have been dead that instant. Instead, I give Grapes a dismissive nod before pushing my way past him.

He follows me, looking for a fight, but one of the

other men calls out, "Cool it, Grapes."

More laughter follows.

Grapes looks like he's about to lose it, but our Drill Sergeant suddenly enters the barracks. Everyone immediately stands at attention at the foot of our beds.

"What's going on here?"

Not a soul speaks.

He gets into the face of the recruit closest to him and growls, "I asked you a question."

"Nothing's going on, Drill Sergeant."

He looks at us all suspiciously. Putting his hands behind his back, he walks down the line of beds, looking sternly at each of us as he passes. At the end of the row, he turns to face us again. "I've had some sorry ass recruits in my day, but this squad exceeds them all."

The room is silent as he walks back to Grapes and stares hard at him. "I don't like you."

Grapes grinds his jaw but says nothing.

The Drill Sergeant continues down the line until he reaches me. "And I'm keeping my eye on you, Walker."

Despite my best intentions, I have not only been noticed by the Drill Sergeant, but also singled out. Now, I will have to work ten times harder to prove myself to the Drill Sergeant, but I'm not worried. I know I can prove myself in this environment.

This is where I say goodbye to the boy I was and become the man I want to be.

A Woman

Cleopatra Cox

The drive to Ethan's house is unusually silent. I'm preoccupied with thoughts about what's about to happen.

I give him a nervous glance and force myself to speak before I chicken out. "I kind of feel dumb asking this right now…"

"What?"

"You've done this before, right?"

"No."

I look at him in shock. "Really?"

He frowns. "Why would I lie about a thing like that, Cleo?"

"It's not that I don't believe you. It's just that…"

"What?"

"It's hard to believe with you being handsome and all."

Ethan snorts in amusement. "Yeah…well, I didn't fit in at the other high school."

I take his hand and squeeze it tightly. "I'm glad you came back then."

Ethan looks back at the road, a smile playing on his lips.

He pulls up to his dad's house and tells me to wait. Then he walks around and opens the door, giving me his hand as support as he helps me jump down onto the sidewalk. "You're almost too tiny for this old truck," he teases.

"No, I'm not." I give him a friendly sock in the arm in protest.

I stare at his house for a moment, knowing this is where I will officially become a woman. Ethan escorts me into the house like the gentleman he is, and I feel chills of anticipation as I walk through the doorway.

"Would you like anything to drink?"

"Got any alcohol?" I venture.

Ethan shakes his head. "My dad is a recovering alcoholic, and I never touch the stuff."

"Smart…" I reply, feeling super embarrassed for suggesting it.

"Are you having second thoughts?" Ethan asks in concern.

"No, I just…have no clue what I'm doing."

"Me either, but I've studied my dad's nudie films to prepare."

"Pornos?"

"Yeah," he chuckles.

I laugh as heat rises to my cheeks. "So, you're telling me you studied them?"

He gives me a crooked grin. "I wanted to make sure

your first time was…special."

Ethan's confession gives me pleasant butterflies. I stand on tiptoe to kiss him on the cheek, but he turns his head toward me and our lips touch.

I gasp softly as his tongue enters my mouth and my body ignites with tingles. I'm more than ready to jump into the unknown with him, confident in his love. "Can we do it now?" I whisper in his ear.

He clears his throat and inadvertently glances down. I notice the rigid outline of his shaft pressing against his jeans. Ethan grabs my hand and leads me into his bedroom. By now, my heart is racing. The first thing I notice is how his bed has been neatly made. Just seeing it makes me weak in the knees.

He looks at me, misreading my emotions. "Look, Cleo, we don't have to do this. It's perfectly okay."

I appreciate how sweet Ethan is being, but I want this, so I sit on his bed. "What do you want me to do?"

His charming grin returns as he sits down beside me. "You don't have to do anything except this…" He places his finger under my chin and kisses me firmly on the mouth, flicking his tongue against my lips.

My body responds to his manly confidence, and I moan lightly as his hand brushes against my breast. While he continues kissing me, he begins unbuttoning my blouse one button at a time. I'm plagued with self-doubt as he pulls back my shirt, suddenly afraid the padded bra will only accentuate how small my breasts are.

I hold my breath as he slips one strap off my shoulder and starts kissing my neck. I am only partially undressed, but I have never felt so naked in my life. There's a thrilling fear in opening myself up to him like this.

Ethan's kisses move lower as he slips off the other strap. With nothing to hold the bra up, it slips down to my waist, leaving my breasts fully exposed to him. I blush in humiliation, but Ethan stares at my chest as if transfixed and mutters, "Oh, my god. You're beautiful…" He begins caressing my breasts as he leans in to kiss me again.

I am on fire for this boy and return his kisses with a passion I can't contain. He groans and pulls away, trying to shift the hard-on being crushed in his dress pants.

"Let me," I offer. I take off my bra and then sink to the floor, kneeling between his legs. Even though I am literally trembling, I reach up and pull on his belt as if I know what I am doing.

Ethan leans back and watches me hungrily as I un-buckle his belt, then unbutton his pants before unzipping them. I pull down his boxers and stare at his manhood. To be honest, I am a little intimidated by how rigid and big it is, but nothing is going to stop me now.

Ethan takes my hand and places it on his hard cock. The moment I touch the smooth skin, he groans loudly.

I am suddenly filled with a sense of power and smile up at him as I lean forward and kiss the round tip. A pearl of clear liquid appears and I'm curious what it will taste like. Without hesitation, I take a quick lick like a little kitten.

Ethan suddenly sits up and cups my face in his hands. "Not another lick. The one thing I couldn't tell from watching those films is how incredible it feels, and I am already on the edge."

He pulls me onto the bed and then stands up to undress. I watch as he pulls off his pants and boxers, followed by his black socks. His white button-up shirt covers his groin area, making for a sexy tease. Ethan slowly undoes his tie and then unbuttons his cuffs before working on the buttons of his shirt, slowly revealing his toned chest to me. I watch with bated breath as he pulls it open for dramatic effect before shrugging it off.

I stare unashamedly at his naked body, turned on by it.

But, I suddenly feel shy again as he lies down beside me. That feeling disappears when he pulls me close and our naked skin touches for the first time. I let out an audible gasp, entranced by the chemistry flowing between us.

Goosebumps rise on my skin as his hand trails over my waist and down my hip, where it finally rests. He's looking at me with a mixture of hunger and devotion.

I feel completely beautiful under his gaze. I lean forward and kiss him, acutely aware of his rigid shaft pressing against my thigh. Although I understand the general mechanics of what is about to happen, I have no idea how he is going to fit, but I am aching inside.

"Ethan…"

I assume he is going to take me when he slips off my skirt and panties. Instead, he moves down between my legs, his face only inches from my sex.

I swallow nervously.

When he looks up at me from between my legs, my

heart skips a beat. "I'm going to need you to tell me how it feels. Remember, I'm new at this."

I giggle as I feel the first light flicks of his tongue on my clit. I bite my lip, unsure if I can handle how ticklish it feels but, as he starts licking and sucking with more intensity, I am overcome with a flood of new sensations. I lay my head back and he stops for a moment. "Too much?"

"Yes, but keep doing it."

He chuckles softly, and I can feel the vibrations of it on my clit. Part of me can't believe he is kissing and licking me there, and another part can't believe we haven't tried this before. There comes a point when he starts licking me with longer strokes of his tongue, like a cat grooming itself. I don't know why, but the rhythmic strokes seem to build on each other, becoming more and more intense as my body anticipates the next lick. I feel like I am going to explode and instinctually clamp my legs shut, trapping his head.

"What?" he asked, wiping his mouth when I release him.

"I need you."

My pussy aches as he climbs onto me. My legs spread wide with his weight between them. I look up into those baby blues, overcome by how much I love Ethan. This isn't two kids experimenting with sex—this is two people desperate to connect with one another.

I watch as he quickly grabs a condom off his nightstand and slides it over his shaft. He then repositions himself, grabbing his cock and pressing the head of it against my small hole. He grits his teeth as he begins to push. As much as I want this, my body resists.

"Kiss me," I tell him.

He leans down and kisses me as he pushes harder. I cry out, feeling a flash of pain as his cock slides into me.

Ethan holds me for a moment before pushing deeper while his tongue claims my mouth. For a moment, I'm in shock and lie still as a tingling sensation takes over my body.

His fervent kisses continue, reigniting my passion. I lift my head to return Ethan's kisses and am rewarded with an even deeper penetration. He braces his arms on the bed and begins to pull out before pushing his shaft back inside me, a low groan escaping his lips as he does so.

His sexual vocalization stirs my desire and makes me even wetter. When he begins slowly stroking me with his cock, I'm in ecstasy. This connection is so incredibly intimate, and more wonderful than I ever imagined.

"I love you, Ethan," I tell him with tears in my eyes.

He stops mid-stroke and says, looking down at me, "I love you."

Ethan is perfect and beautiful.

I wrap my legs around him and cry out in delight as he takes me deeper. He grunts as his thrusts start coming more rapidly.

"Yes, yes," I moan.

Suddenly, he stiffens and every muscle tenses. After several spirited thrusts, he collapses on top of me. "It felt too good. I couldn't stop," he confesses as he lifts his head and looks into my eyes.

Even though my body is still humming with need, I

tell him, "It was wonderful."

Ethan gives me a crooked grin. "I'm not done quite yet." He gets up from the bed and discards the condom in the trash before heading to the bathroom. He returns a short time later with a washcloth in his hand.

Settling down beside me again, he uses a warm cloth to gently clean off the remnants of the blood that marks my deflowering. He then sneaks his hand between my legs and begins playing with my sensitive clit. "Just lie still," he instructs.

I trust him completely, closing my eyes so I can concentrate on his touch. Before I know it, he has rekindled the same feeling his tongue inspired earlier. When it starts to get too much, I shake my head.

"Don't fight it," he tells me. "I want you to feel what I felt."

I struggle against the unfamiliar sensation now challenging my body, but it continues to build with his concentrated attention, and my thighs start to shake.

I whimper as my entire body tenses, reaching some unknown precipice. I stay there as the seconds tick by, but the moment Ethan leans down to kiss me on the lips, my body orgasms in the most exquisite eruption of pleasure I have ever experienced.

I have no control as my hips lift, moving rhythmically up and down as my pussy pulses against his hand.

"It's amazing to watch you come," he growls huskily, kissing me more deeply as the last remnants of my climax pulse to an end.

I look at him in awe when he pulls away. "That was…"

"I know," he says enthusiastically, his eyes flashing with lust. "No wonder everyone wants to fuck all the time." He then looks at me apologetically. "I mean make love."

I giggle.

He pulls me close and wraps me in his arms. "Did I do right by you?"

"Was there ever any doubt?" I answer, smiling at him.

Ethan sighs in satisfaction and we lie there quietly for several moments. He then turns toward me, propping his head on his hand to look at me. "You are the most beautiful woman in the world, Cleopatra Cox."

I love that he's just called me a woman instead of a girl. I grin back at him, amazed by how he makes me feel so beautiful.

He strokes my cheek with a thoughtful expression. "So, I've never asked before, but why did your parents end up naming you Cleopatra? Is it a family name or something?"

I laugh softly, but the memory of it actually makes me sad. "My mom kind of fell into a depression when I was born, so it was left up to Dad to write a name on the birth certificate. He went with Cleopatra because he said it was a strong-sounding name. But, really? Who names a kid that?"

Ethan smiles, gazing into my eyes as if he can read the unspoken pain behind my attempt to play it off. Instead of finding it comforting, it makes me nervous. I'm not used to someone reading me that well. "Needless to say, everyone shortens it to Cleo."

"Cleo," he repeats, saying my name tenderly.

But even when he says it, it sounds masculine in my head which leads me to admit, "Not sure if it was because of my name or just how I was born, but I was a tomboy growing up. Bet you didn't know that about me. I was the kind of girl who didn't mind getting dirty in the mud or scratched climbing a tree."

Ethan smiles, pulling me into his arms. "I wouldn't have suspected that, but I like knowing that about you." He kisses me on the forehead and I sigh in contentment, feeling totally content enfolded in his arms.

"Personally, I wish my dad had named me Claire," I tell him. "It rolls off the tongue and sounds so pretty, don't you think?" I flip over on my stomach, so I am facing him. "I've been thinking of changing my name now that I'm legally old enough."

He chuckles. "You're not a Claire—way too formal."

"What would you call me then?" I asked half-jokingly.

Ethan stares at me tenderly, then shakes his head. "You probably won't like it."

"Can't be any worse than Cleopatra," I assure him.

He smiles as he gently caresses my cheek. "I'd call you Candy."

"Candy," I say in disbelief, surprised he wants to call me by a hooker's name. "Really?"

"Yes," he answers confidently, gazing into my eyes. "You're the sweetest girl I've ever known."

His answer makes me melt inside. Damn, I'm so in love with this boy! "Candy, huh?"

Ethan nods.

"I suppose I could get used to that."

He kisses me on the mouth, gliding his tongue teasingly over my lips. "Yep, you are sweet as can be, Candy…" His eyes flash with desire and he growls huskily, "Are you ready for round two?"

Freedom

Charles Walker

The second week of training is undeniably worse. Not only has our Drill Sergeant added extra activities to our daily routine but, after a morning spent learning how to protect ourselves against a chemical and biological hazard, we are informed we will be facing the gas chamber in the afternoon. I knew this was coming and have tried to mentally prepare myself, but I am still nervous.

I can tell Jackson is too, as he blindly shovels food into his mouth. "I wouldn't scarf down too much. You're probably going to chuck it back up in the gas chamber."

He looks at his tray and sighs, pushing it away from him. "Anything else I should know?"

"Yeah, don't think about it too much, and don't hesitate when we go in."

Jackson shakes his head. "I'm not sure I can make it through this, Walker."

"It's simple," I say to encourage him as much as myself. "We walk in, and they'll tell us to lift our masks one by one so we can state our name, rank, and social security number."

"That's it?"

"Yeah, but take a deep breath before you lift your mask up, and put it back down as soon as you are done."

"I can do that."

"Of course you can." I'm not about to tell him that they will order us to take our masks off before we leave the gas chamber. No need to get him anxious about something he has no control over, although I do add, "No matter what, don't touch your eyes. Trust me on that."

Jackson nods.

After we leave the mess hall, Grapes grumbles, "And how do you know all this fucking shit?"

"I come from a long line of servicemen," I state proudly.

He throws his hands in the air. "No wonder you're such a retard."

All the men sitting around him stiffen, ready to pounce on the prick. "Take that back, Grapes," one of them snarls.

He glances around, realizing his mistake, and mutters, "I meant no offense." When the men aren't satisfied, he says through gritted teeth, "Sorry, BS."

"Yeah, you not only offended my family, but the entire military, Grapes." I can tell the nickname is getting to him.

He glares at me before telling everyone, "Look, I'm

sorry, guys… I'm just busting BS's chops."

I get in his face. "Don't do that again."

He glowers at me but says nothing.

The Army has no tolerance for troublemakers like Grapes. I doubt he will survive another week.

I leave the mess hall on a light stomach, giving some of my anxious teammates a pep talk similar to the one I gave Jackson. It helps me not to dwell on what's coming.

I know it's going to hurt like hell.

When it's time, we are told how to put on our chemical gear and protective mask. Once we're ready, the Drill Sergeant splits us into two groups of five. Unfortunately, my group does not go first, which only intensifies my unease.

I watch Jackson go in first and wait. His group files out minutes later amid a fog of orange gas, coughing violently as snot and tears pour down their faces.

We're next.

I place my right hand on the shoulder of the person in front of me before walking into the chamber. As luck would have it, Grapes is directly behind me. I walk forward into the room still filled with the orangish fog and listen with trepidation as the door shuts behind us. I catch the faint odor of tear gas through my mask and feel the first flutters of panic.

Focusing on my breathing, I wait my turn. When the Drill Sergeant taps my shoulder, I lift my mask up, relying on years of habitually saying my name, rank, and number every day before the bathroom mirror, and loudly state my information to him. I quickly slip the mask back on with minimal discomfort.

Grapes, on the other hand, begins to stutter after he says his name and inadvertently sucks in the gas. He pushes his mask back down.

Once everyone has completed the task, the Drill Sergeant commands, "Before you leave, take off your mask and keep your eyes open until you exit the room."

This is the moment I have been dreading since I was young and learned about the gas chamber, but I dutifully take off my mask. I try holding my breath on the way out, but Grapes grabs onto me in a panic and I inadvertently take in a deep breath.

I drag him with me, the two of us stumbling out of the gas cloud and into the fresh air. Instantly, my eyes burn as if they are on fire and my lungs feel as if they are being torched from the inside out. They swiftly fill up with mucus, which my body forces out.

I immediately hold out my arms as I move away, wanting to distance myself from the lingering gas. I cough so hard I almost retch. Everything burns…

I force my eyes open, knowing it will help, but I feel the overwhelming urge to rub my eyes. To prevent myself from doing that, I raise my arms over my head and clasp my wrists tightly as I take in several ragged breaths.

The searing pain begins to ease.

I look over at Grapes and see he is really suffering as he falls to his knees and retches out the contents of his stomach. "Open your eyes," I tell him, my voice sounding hoarse because my throat is still burning.

He forces his eyelids open and stares at me. His

bloodshot eyes flow with tears. Shaking his head, Grapes rubs his eyes before he can stop himself. He cries out in pain and howls, "Get the fuck away from me, man!"

I turn from him while the others laugh, obviously enjoying his distress.

Although Grapes is the reason I sucked in the gas, I still have a level of sympathy for the prick, knowing how much pain he's in.

Still…it couldn't have happened to a nicer guy.

I head toward Jackson to see how he has fared. The poor kid's skin is bright pink and splotchy—a similar pattern to a Jersey cow. I give him a congratulatory slap on the back. "I see you're still alive and kicking."

"Just barely."

"Well, you did better than Grapes over there," I inform him, pointing at the coughing prick.

Jackson stands a little straighter, obviously pleased he's outshone Grapes.

The Drill Sergeant orders us to assemble, then proceeds to publicly berate each man who failed to give their full information in the chamber. Grapes can't bear the humiliation when he is called out and turns beet red, looking as if he's about to explode when the squad laughs at him.

The Drill Sergeant notices Grapes isn't handling it well and challenges him. "Is the Army too rough for you, Recruit?"

Grapes gives me a hostile glare and shouts, "No, sir!"

The Drill Sergeant walks over to him and gets right up in his face. "What did I tell you about calling me 'sir'?" he growls. "Are you purposely trying to provoke me?"

"No, Drill Sergeant!"

"Drop and beat your face, and when you're done with that set, give me twenty more. Now!"

I stare straight ahead, not wanting to get involved in this. But for some reason, I have incurred the Drill Sergeant's wrath, because he walks over to me next. "I noticed back there that you took particular interest in Recruit Bell."

"No, Drill Sergeant," I answer, desperate not to be associated with the prick.

"Are you calling me a liar?"

"No, Drill Sergeant!"

"I knew there was a reason I didn't trust you."

"You can trust me, Drill Sergeant."

He snarls, "Did I ask for your opinion?"

"No, Drill Sergeant."

I groan inwardly, knowing I'm failing miserably right now.

He moves in close, so we are only inches apart and stares into my eyes, stating ominously, "I don't know what side you are on, Walker."

"I'm on the Army's side, Drill Sergeant." I look at him when I say it, desperate for him to understand how committed I am.

"You're going to prove it. Tonight."

"Yes, Drill Sergeant!" I answer, confident that I will. I'm actually thankful for this opportunity to prove myself to him, even though I know I will pay dearly for it.

After the Non-Commissioned Officer in Charge gives us the rundown for the next day, before we are released to our barracks. Our training day ends at 2000, which is followed by personal time to shit, shower and shave. It's followed by hygiene inspection and lights out at 2100.

As I head out, I see the Drill Sergeant is waiting for me.

"Come with me, Walker," he commands tersely, turning abruptly and walking away.

Jackson nods his encouragement as I hurry to fall in behind. Naturally, Grapes is grinning at me as I pass by, but I pretend not to notice the prick.

I can tell by the Drill Sergeant's stiff gait that he is not happy as he walks out to the training field.

"Drop and give me forty."

As I drop to the ground and begin, he explains, "In case you were wondering, I'm not interested in what brought you to the Army. I don't give a lick about loved ones waiting for you back home. And, I sure in the hell don't give two shits what your future plans are. The only thing I care about is you giving me *everything* you've got for the next eight weeks. Get that, Recruit? Nothing else matters to me."

I look up and nod, his words resonating with me. "Yes, Drill Sergeant." The pain of being disowned by my family, along with the unspoken fear of failing my father, have no place in basic training.

For the next several hours, the number forty becomes my life. I run forty laps, I carry a heavy crate back and forth across the field forty times, I belt out forty renditions of the chorus of "You're a Grand Old Flag", only to end up back at the beginning with forty pushups.

By the time he is done with me, I'm a quivering, sweaty mess with a painfully raspy voice. After looking at his watch, he barks, "We're finished here, Walker. Get up and go hit the fart sack you call a bed."

I immediately stop doing pushups and stand up, nodding to him before heading back to the barracks.

Behind me, I hear one of the other staff address him casually as they pass each other. "Hey, I thought for sure you'd be in bed by now, Marshall. Didn't I hear you just turned forty?"

"Shut up," he grumbles.

Now understanding his obsession with the number, I chuckle under my breath. As I enter the barracks, I can see by the expression on everyone's face that they are amused by my unusual and lengthy punishment.

"Look who's back," Grapes says with a snide grin. "Did you learn your lesson, BS?"

"Yeah," I answer, ripping off my sweaty shirt and throwing it at him. "I learned to stay far the fuck away from you."

I barely have time to get cleaned up before lights out. I settle in my bed, painfully aware of my sore muscles, and wonder if I will be able to sleep. There's no doubt I'm going to hurt for days, but I hold no animosity toward the Drill Sergeant.

Proving myself tonight was not for anyone else's benefit, but mine. I won't waste another second worrying about my father, Grapes, or the future.

I'm committed to living in the moment because it's the only thing I can control. And that knowledge is…

Pure freedom.

Sacrifice

Cleopatra Cox

"Ethan's coming over to spend the afternoon," I tell my dad, giddy with excitement. Normally, I would never dream of having someone over when my mom is in her dark place, but Ethan assures me that my mom's mental state is not a problem—and I love him even more for that.

Dad is flipping pancakes on the stove, and the pleasant sound of them sizzling as they cook fills the air. "Ethan's a good kid," he replies. "You've got a real winner there, C."

His opinion means the world to me and I confess, "Glad you think so, because I plan to marry that man."

My dad puts down his spatula and stares at me. "Don't you think you're rushing things, kiddo?"

"Nope. I've had a crush on Ethan for almost four years now, and you said yourself he's a good catch."

"But you're both still kids."

"Actually, Dad, I'm an adult. If I can join the Army

and die for my country, I think I'm old enough to decide who I want to marry."

Dad chuckles, picking up his spatula again. "As long as you aren't planning on marrying him in the immediate future, I have no problems with Ethan as my future son-in-law."

I get up from the table and give him a one-handed hug as I hand him a plate to put the pancakes on. Together, we return to the table and dish up. I pour an extra amount of maple syrup on my stack, asserting my newly acquired adult status.

Dad doesn't even say a word.

I take a big bite and chew in sweet satisfaction. Glancing briefly at the bedroom door, I swallow it down before asking, "Think Mom will feel the same way?"

"I think it would be good if you told her."

Shrugging, I mumble, "Like she will even hear me…"

He looks at me in concern. "Although we have no idea what's going on in her head, she's still a part of this family and deserves your respect because she's your mother."

I roll my eyes, taking another syrupy bite before answering, "You know I love her, Dad."

He pats me on the head, his smile returning. "You're my sweet girl."

"Girl no more," I insist.

He stares at my plate. "Says the woman with a gallon of syrup on her pancakes."

I giggle, feeling totally in love with life.

I rest my head on Ethan's shoulder as we sit on the couch, spending a lazy afternoon watching college football with my dad. It feels completely normal and comfortable. This is something I've dreamed about for years, and I almost can't believe it's real.

I notice Dad staring at Ethan every now and then, sizing him up now that he's potential husband material. It makes me smile. True, my confession may have been a little premature, but I've known since the day Ethan returned that we were meant to be—it was fated in the stars.

During a commercial, Dad asks out of the blue, "So, Ethan, what are your plans for the future?"

I shake my head, knowing exactly what he's up to.

Poor Ethan…he has no clue I plan to marry him.

"Well, sir, I aim to design custom motorcycles."

"You think there's any money in that?"

Ethan turns to face him and answers, "I hope I can make a living at it but, until I can, I'll work in a garage to make ends meet."

"So, no plans for college?"

"No, sir. I've been told I have talent as a mechanic and don't see the point in spending four years in college when I could be getting real world experience while making money at the same time."

Dad nods his head thoughtfully. "And if Cleopatra decides to go to a traditional college after community college?"

Ethan glances at me with a look of pride. "I'd support whatever she wants, because Cleo will be a success at whatever she does."

"What if it means leaving this place?" my dad prods.

Ethan meets his gaze with confidence. "I've already thought of that, sir. I've got an apprenticeship lined up but, after I'm done there, I'll be able to follow her wherever her career takes her. Mechanic jobs are easy to find. It won't be a problem."

I blush, both surprised and pleased to hear he has planned that far ahead.

Dad glances at the bedroom door. "Now, be truthful with me, son. The fact that C's mother goes through periods like this doesn't concern you?"

Ethan meets his gaze when he answers, "I can see how devoted you are to her."

"Would you be equally devoted to my daughter?"

My stomach twists into a knot. Is my dad trying to compare me to my mother and ruin any chances I have with Ethan?

Ethan looks at me, his expression now serious. "I know Cleo is her own person, with her own set of flaws and weaknesses. Whatever they are, we'll face them together."

I'm deeply touched by his answer and left speechless as I fight back the tears.

When I have regained control, I turn to my dad. "Enough with the questions, Dad." Standing up, I announce to them both, "This girl is in the mood for some ice cream at Handel's."

"They do make a mean mint chocolate chip," my dad

agrees.

"You want to walk there or drive?" Ethan asks, getting up and pulling his car keys out of his pocket.

"Let's walk," I tell him, wanting time alone to talk, afraid my dad's little interrogation might have totally freaked him out.

Ethan stuffs the keys back into his pocket and takes my hand instead. "We'll make a date of it."

Oh my, do I blush! Is it even possible to fall more in love with the guy?

As we head out the door, Ethan calls back to my dad, "Don't worry, Mr. Cox. I'll pick you up a pint of that mint while we're there."

"Thanks, kid."

After the door closes, I look at Ethan in concern. "I'm so sorry about that. I apologize for Dad hammering all those questions at you."

He shrugs. "I kind of liked it because it means he sees me in your future."

I press myself against him and smile so hard my cheeks hurt.

As the two of us walk down the sidewalk, I'm filled with a profound sense of well-being. Everything seems right with the world, and I just want to shout my happiness to the world—but that would be weird.

Ethan leans over and presses the button for the crosswalk while we watch all the cars speeding by. As we wait, he casually puts his arm around my waist, and it makes my stomach flutter. We feel so good together, as if we've been a serious couple for years.

"I love you," I blurt, too happy to keep it inside.

He leans down, giving me a quick peck on the lips just as the light changes. "I love you too, Candy." Grasping my hand tightly, the two of us walk across the street together.

I secretly hope all the people watching from the cars can tell just how in love we are.

I turn my head when I hear a strange, high-pitched screech and freeze when I see a huge pickup truck barreling down on us, sparks and flames spewing from its sides. Before I can even react, Ethan pushes me forcefully out of the way.

I fly out of the path of the oncoming truck and almost get knocked out when my head crashes into the pavement. I lie there momentarily, confused by the horrifying sound of crunching metal and breaking glass that fills the air.

I force my head to turn, blinking several times in disbelief as I watch a flaming wheel roll by me in slow motion.

Ethan…

I fight to get up, but as soon as I try to sit up, everything goes black.

As if in a dream, I hear frantic voices and feel myself being lifted up. I force my eyes open and cry out for Ethan.

"You're going to be okay," an EMT tells me in a comforting tone as I'm rolled on a gurney toward an ambulance.

"Ethan…" I cry out again hoarsely. My mouth is dry and my tongue swollen.

I look around desperately, hoping to catch sight of

him.

My world ends the moment I spot the limp body on the other side of the street—covered in a white sheet.

Ethan…

I can't feel him.

I lie here in the dark, the pain so terrible, I can't breathe.

Tears run down my face, but I am numb, body and soul. I feel his loss like a physical wound—bloody and gaping.

As if from a great distance, I hear my dad's voice. "C, I need you to eat something."

A warm spoon presses against my lips, but I have no will to open them.

"Please, you need to eat."

After several failed attempts, I hear him get up and leave my bedroom.

I rock myself afterward, haunted by the knowledge that Ethan sacrificed himself to save me. If I hadn't insisted on walking that day, he'd still be alive.

I killed you…

I writhe in pain with that knowledge.

Oh God, it hurts!

I just need this pain to end.

There's a loud crash and the sound of tinkling of glass hitting the floor on the other side of my bedroom door. It instantly takes me back to that moment just after the crash, and a scream erupts from deep inside me.

My dad comes running in. "I'm sorry, C. I didn't mean to scare you, sweetheart. I just had a little accident in the kitchen…"

An unfamiliar tone in his voice stirs something inside me—I can sense his fear. For the first time since coming home from the hospital, I push myself to leave the cocoon of darkness I've enveloped myself in.

Blinking several times, I force myself to "see" again and turn my gaze toward my father. I croak out one word, "Dad…"

He gasps when our eyes meet. "You're back."

Dad's clutching his bloody hand, which he's wrapped in a kitchen towel.

"What happened?"

He looks at his hand and shakes his head. "When I was putting the dishes away, I knocked the glass mixing bowl down. I tried to catch it as it fell out of the cupboard, but I wasn't fast enough and only managed to grab the glass shards as it hit the marble counter."

During his short explanation, the towel had become completely soaked with blood. "You need to see a doctor," I tell him, the protective side of me forcing its way to the surface. I force myself to get out of bed, ignoring the emotional pain that smothers me like a death shroud.

"Don't worry about it, C. The only thing that matters is that you've come back," he states.

As much as I want to escape back into the darkness, I can't stand to see my dad hurt. I slowly walk to the bathroom with him, so I can get a better look at his injury.

Washing off the blood, I see he has a long, but clean, cut down the side of his palm. I grab gauze from the medicine cabinet and tell him to press hard against the wound to stop the bleeding while I get the medical tape and disinfectant.

After the bleeding is under control, I bandage his hand. He walks me out to the living room and asks me to sit on the couch. The same couch Ethan and I were sitting on that day…

I look around the room and feel disoriented. Everything that's familiar now seems so foreign and wrong to me because Ethan is gone.

I glance at my mother's door, seeing that it is still shut.

My eyes shift to my own bedroom door, feeling its call to return and escape this choking pain.

But, when I look over at my dad, I can see the concern in his eyes. I swallow down the urge to escape, knowing he's had to take care of both of us on his own.

I have never wanted to be like my mother but, in my grief, I was becoming her. I knew how hard it was to be among the ones left behind, having experienced it repeatedly with my mom while growing up—I can't do that to him.

No matter how much I need to…

"I'm back for good, Dad," I assure him.

The look of relief on his face is heartbreaking to see.

The fighter inside me awakes, and I silently vow to God and the world not to give in to that urge again, no matter what the future holds.

"How long has it been?" I ask him hesitantly, having no concept of the time that has passed.

"You've been in your room since you came home six weeks ago."

I cringe at hearing his answer. "That long?"

"You were inconsolable after Ethan died."

Even now, I feel my heart crushing in on itself, hearing those words.

I remember clearly Ethan pushing me away, but everything after that is a blur. I want to understand. I *need* to understand.

"What happened? Why did that truck head straight toward us?"

My dad takes my hand and squeezes it. "Are you sure you want to talk about it?"

I nod, even as I feel my throat constricting in pain while a flood of emotions threatens to overtake me. "I know Ethan saved my life."

"He did," my dad answers with a look of sympathy. "And I am eternally grateful to him for that."

I close my eyes. Ethan would be alive if it weren't for me.

"We don't need to do this now," my dad suggests.

I open my eyes and gaze into his. "I can't run away any longer."

Even now, I hear the strange squeal of the truck as it barrels straight toward us, and I ask him, "What was wrong with the truck? Why was it trying to hit us?"

"Oh, C…" he says, his voice full of sadness. "The driver was drunk and had been running from the cops for over an hour before he reached you. By that time, he'd already hit several cars and lost a tire in one of the collisions."

That explains the flames.

"So, Ethan died for nothing…" My voice trails off as I swallow down this horrible truth, unable to wrap my head around the fact that Ethan's death was preventable.

"He's dead because some guy decided to get toasted in the middle of the day and get into his truck?"

"I'm afraid so," my dad answers with tears in his eyes.

"How many other people died because of this man?"

"No one else—only minor injuries."

"Except for Ethan," I sob.

My dad gathers me in his arms, trying to comfort me. "I'm so sorry, C."

"It's not fair!" I cry, my heart shattering into a million pieces all over again.

"No, sweetheart, it's not."

Dad holds me close as I finally mourn the loss of my Ethan.

I will never hear his voice again or see his smile or feel his arms around me…

Buddy

Charles Walker

I've become a new man under the abrasive but thoughtful instruction of my Drill Sergeant. I can tell he actually wants me to succeed, and that knowledge makes me feel invincible.

I should have known that would be short-lived.

Everything is going well until the Drill Sergeant tells us he's assigning us a battle buddy for the remainder of training.

I have looked forward to this day and stand at attention, waiting for my assignment, hoping for Jackson. While he still lacks confidence, Jackson and I are a good fit and I know we will do well together.

I have to hide my disappointment when he is paired up with another recruit. I keep my cool as I look over the men left, but my hope is short-lived.

"Walker, you've been assigned with Bell."

I see that the Drill Sergeant is watching me intently, so I hold back any sign of displeasure and answer confidently, "Yes, Drill Sergeant."

But Grapes has no discipline and growls under his breath, "Fuck!"

I want to roll my eyes as I watch the Drill Sergeant walk over to him. "That's three laps around the track, and you'll give me forty pushups on your return."

The Drill Sergeant then looks at me. "You heard me."

I clench my jaw, now realizing that I get to share in any punishment my buddy receives. Without wasting time to think about it, I head to the track to start my laps.

Why, of all people, did the Drill Sergeant pair me up with Grapes? We could not be more polar opposite, and we don't even like each other.

Grapes passes me on the track, muttering, "Asshole."

"Save your breath, Grapes," I reply, easily passing him. I may have to take his punishments, but I am *not* going to let him beat me. He speeds up and we make a full-on sprint back to the squad, dropping to the ground at the same time. To my great satisfaction, I finish first and stand up, breathing hard from the effort as he finishes up his last two pushups.

"Wipe that grin off your face, Walker!" the Drill Sergeant shouts at me as he walks over. "There should be no look of pride after punishment."

I immediately frown. "Yes, Drill Sergeant."

He walks over to Grapes. "And you let him beat you."

Grapes' eyes flash with anger as he glances over at

me.

With those simple words, our Drill Sergeant has set the groundwork for an intense rivalry.

I'm not about to let that prick ruin everything I'm working for, and I will do whatever it takes to set his sorry ass straight.

That evening, the drill instructor comes in to call out the names of everyone who has received mail. I already know he won't be calling my name, but every time, I still hold out hope.

I'm not the only who has yet to hear their name. Grapes is equally letter-less.

It is a sad reality we both share but, unlike him, I continue to write a letter home every Tuesday. The routine has several purposes. It acts as a running record of my experiences here, as well as forcing me to reflect back on my week.

But the main purpose is to let Jacob know I have not forgotten him.

After the sergeant leaves, I pick up my pen and start on my letter.

"You're pathetic," Grapes growls from his bunk. "At least I don't grovel. It only makes you look like a chump."

I glance at him dismissively. "A least I have someone to write home to." I return my attention to the blank paper and start scribbling.

Hey Jacob,

I made it through the gas chamber and become acquainted with the M-16 I'll be using throughout training. I can't tell you how good it felt to hold one again, even if it's old and abused.

Right now, the squad is learning how to hold, point, take apart, clean, and put the gun back together. Funny, since you and I can do that in our sleep.

The big news this week is that I got my Battle Buddy assignment. I find it ironic that he is the last person I wanted to be paired with.

Thing is, Jacob, life works like that. You can either get pissed about it or you can face it head on. I've wanted to see this jerk go for a while now based on his crappy attitude but, now that I'm stuck with him, I'm going to make sure he sticks it out to the end.

Everything is a matter of perspective.

So if things are getting you down, little man, I want you to keep that in mind. Don't waste energy getting mad. Harness that energy to get through it. Learn that and you'll go far in life.

Hope you are having fun this summer. Give Mama a hug for me.

Love,
Charlie

Folding up the letter, I set it down while I fish out an envelope from my locker. I don't see Grapes sneaking up to grab it before it's too late. "What do we have here? A love letter to the girl that left you for a better man?"

I rush over to him, trying to get it back as he starts reading. "'Hey Jacob…' Oh, is that how you roll? I'm going to have to report you to the proper authorities."

The other men are now curious to hear the rest, so they grab my arms and hold me back.

Grapes continues reading it out loud and stops after I mention being able to do it in our sleep. "Oh, I *bet* you two can do it in your sleep," he says in a sarcastic tone.

"He's my brother, asshole," I snarl, trying to break the hold they have on me.

"Right…"

The other men laugh at my expense, but I don't care what anyone thinks. I just want to get that damn letter back before he reads any more.

"Now, this should be good," Grapes says eagerly. "'The big news this week is that I got my Battle Buddy assignment…'" Grapes reads the next few lines to himself and then looks at me and frowns.

"What does it say?" one of guys holding me demands.

Grapes crumples the letter. "Doesn't matter."

Another guy snatches it from him and continues reading as people elbow each other while listening to my thoughts about my Buddy assignment. The guy trails off after reading, "'Give Mama a hug for me…'" Everyone is silent as he hands the crinkled letter back to me with a sheepish expression.

The guys look away, unwilling to look me in the eye—all except Grapes, who is fuming.

I glare back at him. "If anyone has a problem with me writing to my little brother, be sure to see me outside so we can *discuss* it."

I despise having my private thoughts shared with everyone, but I keep my cool as I smooth out the letter and start copying it onto another piece of paper.

Grapes is in a foul mood the next day and takes out his frustration on me by purposely disobeying the Drill Sergeant's orders. I know what he's doing, and I will not lose to that prick. Every time we get punished, I make sure I am the first one done, which only infuriates Grapes more.

The entire squad feels the pain when the Drill Sergeant starts dishing out the punishment to the group to force him to fall in line. Nobody likes Grapes by the end of the day but, being his buddy, I get the heat too.

Several of the guys surround me in the barracks. "You should fucking let him win so we can be done with this. What does it matter, anyway?"

"It matters to me, damn it! I'm not the one getting in trouble, but I'm the one paying for it. The only recourse I have is to beat him."

"But you know it pisses him off, and now you're getting us involved too."

"I didn't come to the Army to baby another recruit's

ego. He's the one you have problems with, so go deal with him."

"But your need to win is causing this," another insists.

"What do you think will happen if I suddenly let him beat me now? You think he'll be satisfied? No, it'll only make things worse. Trust me."

"What are you going to do about it?" Jackson asks me after they leave unsatisfied.

"There's only one thing I can do." I walk up to Grapes and point at the door. "You. Me. Now."

We exit the barracks quietly. The other men know this is going to be a good fight, but they stay put, unwilling to risk further punishment.

I head to the side of the building where we won't be seen and face him. I speak in a low whisper, so we won't be heard, "I'm ready to knock some sense into that thick skull of yours."

Grapes doesn't waste a second and throws a punch. I easily block it and follow up with a side jab. His eyes flash with rage as he turns to face me, matching my low tone in order to avoid detection. "You want me out, but you don't get to fuck with my life, asshole."

"You bet I do, but now I'm stuck with you because our drill sergeant has a sick sense of humor."

He snorts. "Yeah, I see the way you suck up to him. Don't think the rest of us haven't noticed."

"If following commands is your idea of sucking up, then yes, I'm guilty."

His expression turns ugly. "*Everything* you say is bullshit. Is that why your family doesn't write back?"

I hit him square in the face.

"Hit a nerve, did I?" He grins, rubbing his chin.

"Nobody writes you either, prick, and I bet it has something to do with your winning personality."

Grapes throws another punch, but I dart out of the way. I've sparred plenty of times with my father and I'm confident in my ability to fight.

He starts walking around me slowly like a predatory animal looking for his chance to strike. "Noticed you didn't mention a father in that letter. Is that because Daddy split the scene when you appeared? I bet he did."

"This isn't about my family, prick," I hiss.

"Maybe your father killed himself and you're the reason why."

Even though I know he's trying to provoke me, I take a swing. He blocks it and follows through with a solid hit to my gut.

I back away and start bouncing on the balls of my feet as I move side to side, suddenly realizing I might have a real fight on my hands. This could be good. I need to release my pent-up anger, and it appears Grapes is offering himself up as a sacrifice.

"I bet your father wishes you were dead," he says.

I narrow my eyes, his words hitting a little too close to home. Waiting for my opening, I deliver another punch to his face and watch him stagger from the impact.

"You're easy to read..." he tells me with a grin, wiping the blood from his face.

"Not as easy as you are to hit." I give him a quick jab to the ribs.

Grapes isn't light on his feet, so he lowers his head and barrels straight at me, throwing me to the ground. After a couple of hits to the face, I'm back on my feet.

I love the adrenaline rush and goad him further. "I bet you've failed at everything you've tried."

Grapes snarls ominously. Once we finally connect, it gets brutal. I take my rage against my father out on him, while he unleashes his fury against the world on me.

We are so focused on each other, we don't realize we've been spotted by a passing Drill Instructor. He immediately breaks the fight up and we are ordered to return to our barracks to await punishment.

We both know it will be harsh.

However, as we stand there waiting, with our faces bloody and bruised, a feeling of comradery prevails—and in that moment, we become friends.

New Friend

Candy

I sit in class, trying to keep my eyes open, but algebra is horrifically boring.

Even in a college setting, being taught by a real professor, can't make those numbers any more interesting. Part of me regrets taking this class, but I need the routine to fill up the empty hours of my life.

I'm taking basic courses my first year of college—the ones I know I can pass without trying. It doesn't matter if I learn something or not, because the classes help me not to mourn Ethan's death every second of every day.

I've chosen a college out of state, away from the memories that threaten to swallow me whole. It hasn't been easy on my dad, but Mom has returned to the land of the living. With me out of the house, they can live a normal life—and I can begin a new one.

The day I made the decision to leave, I cut my hair short and dyed it blonde. It's the physical embodiment of this fresh start, and I've even gone a step further by legally changing my name in honor of Ethan.

Nobody knows why I changed my name to Candy, not even my parents. But when I look in the mirror and see the new me, I know Ethan was right.

I *am* Candy.

After classes, I normally go to the library to study and don't return to my dorm room until after dinner. My roommate is far too chatty, and even though I like her, I can't stand her incessant gossiping.

Who cares what so and so said, or what so and so did? I sure don't.

So, I sit in the quiet sanctuary of the campus library and surf the Internet to fill up the time. I've visited every site known to man, and have seen a few things that I can't unsee, but I don't regret it.

The best part for me are the intelligent discussions I can have with people around the world. To be completely alone, but not feel alone, is miraculous.

Because I jump from site to site, I don't tend to see the same people, but I have noticed one person named Liege who seems to show up a lot on the threads. While we don't agree on most things, I find his posts provoking and enjoy reading them.

I'm not looking for personal interaction, but all that changes while reading a post about Google being named the world's most popular email service. I see that Liege has left a comment bashing the service and claiming Google has risen too quickly and will disappear in less than five years.

I laugh to myself because I disagree and start typing my rebuttal. As soon as I post it, I get a new message in

Gmail—from him.

It freaks me out a little and I'm hesitant to open it, since this is the first personal contact I have received from people I've only come across on the Internet. I find the emotional distance comforting.

But the longer the email sits there, the more curious I become. Based on his account information, I know he lives in another state which means there's no chance of meeting him in real life.

So, with some trepidation, I click on his message.

Hey Candy,

I have noticed you around and wanted to reach out personally. I enjoy reading your comments and think you would like this other site I'm on.

If you are interested, let me know and I'll send the link.

Liege

After reading his simple note, I feel at ease. The guy seems nonthreatening, and the fact he hasn't included the link means he is giving me the choice to respond. I appreciate that.

After debating with myself, I decide to type a message back.

Liege,

Appreciate the email. I've enjoyed your posts, as well, and am interested in the site you mentioned. Please send the link.

Candy

I look it over, feeling satisfied it reflects a similar noncommittal tone. After hesitating for several seconds, I hit Send and wait.

When I don't get a response back after an hour, I pack up my backpack and head to the dorm. I'm actually glad he hasn't answered because it keeps the emotional distance I crave, but I'm even more curious about the discussion site he wants me to join.

It's three days later and I have yet to get a reply, even though I've seen a few new posts from him on different sites.

I'm wondering if he's changed his mind, preferring to remain impersonal. I don't mind. It's not like I was the one to reach out first.

But, just as I'm about to leave the library, I see his email pop up. I waste no time opening it.

Candy,

You seem like an intelligent woman, and it takes intelligence to have an open mind. Here is the link I promised.

www.inthelifestyle.com

Let me know what you think.

Liege

The name of the website itself has me wondering, so I click on the link and am taken to a site with multiple discussion topics.

As I read them over, though, a chill runs down my spine. "I'm not in Kansas anymore..." I mutter to myself.

One of the other college students turns her head and looks at me.

I blush. If only she could see what I'm seeing...

The topics of discussions range from Masters and Slaves, Group Fun, Training Your Sub for Service, to actual classified ads: Submissives and Owners Seeking Partners.

I don't realize I've stopped breathing until the blood starts to pound in my head.

This guy is into some seriously crazy shit!

Just to be sure, I look back over his two emails to convince myself I haven't missed something in his messages.

He seemed so normal...

I never guessed there were websites like this, where people openly advertise wanting to be owned by other people. What the heck?

Not one to shy away from uncomfortable topics, I do what Liege probably suspected I would do.

I start reading some of the posts.

Nothing is sexier than when my Master takes me to the club and plays with me in front of other people. There is just something hot about being watched while he puts me through my paces.

nymph

Although I can't imagine doing that myself, I can see it being exciting for some people and don't find it shocking.

Looking through another discussion, I read:

Subspace is what I live for now. I don't care how I get there. I just want to experience it again and again. Who knew it could be such fun?

bunny

I am clueless what she is talking about, but it's obvious that whatever *it* is must feel amazingly good.

Okay…my curiosity has been officially piqued.

I move to the discussion about Masters and Slaves and see this post:

If my sub is being particularly bratty, I make her lie on the bed and tie her up while she explains to me what she's done wrong. I then take off my belt and make her kiss it before I begin punishing her.

I find it helpful to have her bound so she can't move when I deliver her punishment, and I don't stop until there are tears.

Master Ian

My jaw drops.

I can't even imagine…

I'm about to click out of the site when these simple words catch my eye.

I love my pet.

Even though that last post freaked me out...this seems sweet, so I click on the post.

> **During the day, I get pulled in every direction at my job, but when I come home and find my pet waiting for me—all the day's stress falls away.**
>
> **She is so beautiful, kneeling on the floor as she looks up at me, wearing only her jeweled collar around her neck.**
>
> **Knowing that her greatest desire is to please her Master never fails to excite me. Love my little kitten.**
>
> **Drake**

I stare at this post for a long time. The tenderness in his declaration stirs something profound inside me. I can see myself kneeling on the floor, a pretty collar around my neck, waiting for someone to come home.

It wouldn't be what I had with Ethan—what we had can never be replaced.

But this could be new and different, a fresh start.

I smile as I click out of the site and go back to the email Liege sent. He must be wondering if I've received it and how I will react.

Since he made me wait a couple of days, I decide to follow suit, not wanting to come across desperate or something. However, I definitely want to discuss this further with him.

As I leave the library, I start looking at the other college students as they walk by. Are any of them leading this secret life? It's as if a whole new world I never knew existed has been revealed to me.

The idea of it intrigues me so much that I find myself gravitating to the pet section the next time I'm at the store, and I start looking at the cat collars with a more critical eye. I even pick one up and find a mirror, so I can see how it looks against my neck.

"Do you need help?" a store employee asks as she approaches me.

I blush, quickly pulling the collar away from my neck. "I was just looking at the size to see if it would fit my dog."

"Oh, if you're looking for dog collars, they're one aisle down."

"Great," I answer meekly, thoroughly embarrassed as I put the cat collar back and move to the next aisle. I end up grabbing a random collar and telling her thanks as I head to the front to buy it.

Now I own a dog collar, and I don't even have a dog.

I wait to answer his email two days later.

Dear Liege,

I have to admit I was a little thrown by the website you linked. But, like you said, it's important to keep an open mind so I started exploring it a little.

While there are a lot of things I don't understand, I certainly found it informative.

What's your take on this site?

Candy

I'm pleased with my email. I'm not giving up too much information about myself and throwing the ball back into his court at the same time.

To my delight, I get an answer the very next day.

Candy,

Good to hear you have an open mind. You asked my take on the site without stating your own. Rather than waste time going back and forth, let me be frank with you.

I am a Dominant.

Let me answer the question I'm sure you want to ask. I am looking for an online submissive, and I thought you would make a good candidate.

I await your reply.

Liege

My heart beats rapidly as I read his email and then read it again.

Liege is a Dominant…

I'm not entirely sure what that entails but, after looking at the site, I surmise it's the same as a Master. I feel tingles of excitement knowing a Master is actually talking to me and thinks I'd be a good match.

Even though the whole BDSM thing kind of frightens me, it sure would be great as a distraction. Way better than algebra!

This whole week, I haven't had to drag myself out of bed. The fact that he is only looking for an online relationship makes it feel safe—a way for me to escape the pain without risking anything.

Dear Liege,

I know nothing about this lifestyle and am not even sure what you are asking of me.

I need more details about what's involved before I can give you a simple yes or no. However, I will say that I'm fascinated that this hidden world exists and am flattered that you asked me.

Please keep in mind I'm a college student and have to put my studies first.

Candy

Liege takes a day to respond but, when I open his email, I can tell it's definitely been worth the wait.

Candy,

I suspected you were new to the lifestyle, which means I need to take on the role as your trainer and Master.

To do this, I will give you tasks to complete at the beginning of each week, and you will report back to me at the end. This should not interfere with school.

However, once you start down this path with me, you will find it difficult to think of anything else. I plan to start you out with small tasks and build up to more challenging ones—that's when it

starts to get fun.

Once you make the decision to become my submissive, I want you to respond with an email entitled "Task 1 Complete" and attach the picture in the email.

From that point forward, you will address me only as Master.

A BDSM relationship is based on trust. This is not a game you play whenever it pleases you. This is a commitment to me—and to yourself.

Before I can reveal your pet name, you must complete my first task.

Task 1

When you are ready to train as a submissive, write "Yes, Master" on a piece of paper using your lipstick, then take a picture of yourself holding it up as you look at the camera.

Liege

His task seems easy enough, although I'm curious as to why the message needs to be written in lipstick. The way he talks about starting me out slow and BDSM being about trust makes me feel good, but what *really* gets my heart racing is the fact he already has a pet name picked out for me—and I hadn't even mentioned anything about that to him.

It feels as if he can read my mind!

As I gather my books and stuff them into my backpack, along with my laptop, I already know I am going to say yes but I decide to sleep on it.

I leave the library with a bounce in my step. Already,

I am thinking about what Liege looks like and what kind of things he will ask me to do.

Who knew being bossed around could be fun?

I fluff up my hair one last time and glance at the picture of Ethan smiling at me.

In my heart, I know he would be happy I am moving on, but not trying to replace him.

Ethan will forever be my first and only love.

I take a picture of myself and groan when I look at it. I need it to be perfect for this first task. After ten more tries, I finally have one I like. This will be the first time Liege has seen a close-up of me. As my profile picture, I have one of me pushing against an impossibly huge rock as my profile pic.

It represents how I feel, but it's too small to really see my face.

Rather than a picture, Liege has some kind of ancient symbol as his profile pic, so I have zero idea what he looks like, but I kind of like not knowing—it adds to his whole Dominant mystique. Besides, what a person looks like shouldn't matter. It's what's on the inside that counts.

I have to laugh at myself as I decide to take one more picture. For all my high talk about looks not mattering, I'm sure putting a lot of energy into getting this one just right. When I'm finally satisfied, I get out my laptop and hit Reply.

After attaching the photo, I start typing.

Dear Master,

Okay, that feels weird—even just typing it.

I stare at it for a while, questioning if I am really ready to go through with this. But, when I think about how boring and depressing my life was before Liege, I realize I can't turn back now.

The task is complete. I hope it meets your expectations.

I'm so new at this, I am relying on your understanding if I do something wrong.

You're right. We haven't even begun and I can't stop thinking about what things you will have me do, especially with us being so far apart.

To be honest, I'm a little apprehensive because BDSM seems a bit scary, but you've got me curious. Plus, I'm dying to know what name you've picked out for me.

Candy

I hesitate, my finger hovering over the Send button. I'm about to make a commitment to someone I have never met.

This seems crazy.

However, Liege has stirred something inside of me I never knew existed.

This isn't about love; this is about escape.

I push the button and sit back.

For better or worse, I have a Master now.

Welcome Home

Charles Walker

The day of our graduation from basic training, I stand proudly next to Grapes and Jackson. None of us has failed basic training due to the brilliant, but punishing, guidance of our leader.

Drill Sergeant Herbert Marshall has molded us from boys to men in nine short weeks.

We are U.S. Army Soldiers now.

Grapes and I watch as Jackson's family come up to congratulate him. I think of that nervous kid I met on the bus. He stands taller and with a confident air—no longer needing to scratch the back of his neck. You can tell his parents are impressed by his stepfather's proud smile and the way his mother keeps staring at him with a look of awe.

Grapes and I stand alone and vow to drink heavily tonight.

"Feels good, sitting on the sidelines, doesn't it?" he jokes.

"I won't lie. I wish my family was here."

Grapes shakes his head. "I'm glad mine aren't."

I stick out my hand and say in a fatherly voice, "I'm damn proud of you, son."

He chuckles, taking on the same tone as he shakes it. "You may not be good enough, but you're good enough for the Army, son."

We both laugh.

I was hoping to see Jacob and my mom, and I am disappointed they are not here, but it's not entirely unexpected. There's no point in dwelling on it. Besides, we're all headed for Advanced Individual Training after this, but only two of us are doing field artillery training. It's a damn good thing I've made my peace with Grapes, because it appears I'm stuck with the prick.

My goal has always been to protect those who fight for our country, and I will do what it takes to rise up in the ranks as fast as I can. I may not have a college education, but I have the bullheaded determination of a Walker, and I know my destiny.

That night, despite the fact I have never received a response, I write to my little brother.

Hey Jacob,

I graduated from boot camp today and am officially in the US Army. I can't tell you how good it feels!

I'm missing Mama's warm rolls and watching Welcome Back, Kotter with you Thursday nights. But really, I'm just missing spending time with you guys. I look forward to making up for it when we get together.

I know you only have a few more weeks of summer, so play hard.

But after school starts, hit those books just as hard, little man.

I'll be writing you again after my first week of field artillery training. I'll let you know how that goes.

Oh, and Grapes, my Battle Buddy, says hello.

Love,
Charlie

I show Grapes the last line in my letter. "I figure he should know you made it."

There's a slight smile on his lips when he elbows me in the ribs. "No thanks to you, BS."

He deserves to be remembered for this accomplishment, which is why I included him in Jacob's letter. It will be a record of his achievement, even if his own family never hears of it.

Grapes has come a long way, and *no one* should be forgotten.

Seven Years Later

It's pitch black out, not a star in the sky. A perfect night for a live fire exercise. The tension in the platoon is high, but I know my men and trust in their training.

Dividing them into squads, I explain team objectives and how they will aid in the success of our mission. It won't be easy. The battlefield is filled with mortar pits, barbed wire, tank traps, and trenches. I am acting as the gunner to ensure they make it to the objective without incident.

Using a stick, I draw out in the dirt where each group is to go. It's simple enough, but I know what they are in for and tell them, "You have been trained for this. Stay focused. Don't overthink it."

The moment they head out, machine guns start blasting. The sky is so dark, I can't see my men moving along the ground. I only get a glimpse of them when the parachute flares are launched lighting up the entire battlefield.

Damn, their progress is slow. But I have faith in my men and my plan.

My part tonight is to use a mortar gun to destroy the targets once my team finds them. When it's time, I double-check the angle and azimuth, knowing my math needs to be spot on or I'll miss.

I yell, "Hang it!" and aim the mortar gun before the shell is dropped into the shaft. "Fire!" A thrill runs through me when I watch as our first target is destroyed.

We move on to the next stage of our mission, but total darkness and the stench of gunpowder is messing with the minds of my men below and it's slowing us down. When a flare goes off, I see several groups huddled together with their hand on the man in front of them to keep from getting lost in the dark while others are being held back, tangled in barbed wire. But, as I watch, each squad clears their hurdles and gets where they need to be.

All of my men are in "soldier mode" now, their intense training taking over as they react to the environment around them. They have only the objective in mind. Their ability to act without having to think brings order in the midst of chaos.

The deafening boom of the artillery shells fill the night air as yet another one of our target is destroyed.

I feel a rush of adrenaline, watching it blow up. This is what I was born for.

Another flare shows me that my men are close to our final objective. One last hill. One last target. Finished. Mission completed. I rush over and join my men, my heart swelling with pride at their victory.

My platoon has performed well under the pressure of our live fire exercise, and I am confident they are prepared for real battle.

I've had a bad feeling about returning home…

When my two-year enlistment ended, my First Lieutenant advised me to take time off to get my associate degree. Impressed by my performance and initial ASVAB score, he informed me that a few years earlier, at the end of the Vietnam War, the Army began allowing enlisted men with the degree to enroll in Officer Candidate School.

I took advantage of the opportunity, joining an accelerated program to get my associates degree as rapidly as possible to attend OCS and earn my commission as Second Lieutenant. By pushing myself hard, and using all of my personal leave for classes, I attained the remaining credits needed for my Bachelor of Science degree several years later.

All that hard work and persistence finally paid off when I became First Lieutenant.

I now have my eyes set firmly on reaching my goal of Captain within the next two years. However, in all this time, I have yet to hear a word from my family. My high school buddy, Will, confirms they still live at the same house, so I continue to send letters to Jacob every Tuesday. It's the only thread of connection I have with my family, and I can't give that up.

I know Jacob has just finished his first year of high school—I can't even picture him being that old.

It's time I come home.

I step out of the taxi, dressed in my service uniform, and grab my duffle bag from the seat before handing the driver his cash. I then turn to face the house.

It looks exactly the same, not one blade of grass out of place. My father has always been fastidious about keeping the yard and exterior pristine, while my mother is expected to keep the same standard inside.

I feel a sense of comfort as I stare at our house.

Even though seven years have passed, it looks as if time has stood still. I, on the other hand, have changed dramatically. I am not the same person I was when I left—too much has happened since then.

One of Jacob's friends passes by on his bike and shouts out as he whizzes by, "Heya, Charlie. Welcome home!"

I turn to him and wave. "Thanks, kid."

I stare at the house again, building up my courage before heading up the walk. Before I make it to the porch, my father comes out and shuts the door behind him. "I told you not to come back."

I take off my hat out of respect and state, "It's been seven years, sir."

"What difference does that make? I told you the minute you left this house, you weren't to come back here."

"How is that fair to Jacob or Mom?"

"Your mother and I are agreed on this, and what Jacob thinks has little relevance."

I shake my head, unable to believe he could be this unforgiving and stubborn. I know my mother does not agree but is afraid to confront him, and it's Jacob who is suffering the most for it.

I put my hat back on. "I am a First Lieutenant of the U.S. Army and have been gone seven years serving our country, sir. I have a right to see my brother."

I hear a car pull up behind me and turn to look. I'm shocked to see a police officer step out from a cop car and realize my father called the police before coming outside.

The officer strolls up the walk, saying, "I just happened to be passing by and got a call. What seems to be the problem here, Mr. Walker?"

"This man is trespassing," my father barks.

I look at the officer and explain, "I've just come to see my family."

The officer looks at my father with a confused expression. "Is this your son?"

"No," my father states firmly.

This is the first time he has verbally denied me as his son in front of another. It cuts deep.

"I want this man off my property now!" my father demands.

The officer gives me a sympathetic look and glances at the decorations on my uniform. "I'm sorry, Lieutenant Walker, but I'm going to have to ask you to leave."

I glare at my father. "I can't believe you're doing this. I've done nothing to deserve it, *Father.*"

He snorts. "You are no son of mine."

The neighbors have come out to see what's going on, curious about the police car and the commotion my father is causing.

I turn to the officer. "I have no interest in causing a scene. I simply came to see my little brother."

The man presses his lips together and turns to look at my father in disbelief. "At least let him say goodbye to the boy."

My father roars at me, "Go, and never set foot on this property again!"

I nod to the officer and turn to walk away. My father has won. I will never come back here.

The officer walks beside me and asks, "You need a

ride, Lieutenant Walker?"

"A ride to the nearest bar would be great."

"You got it," he replies, opening the passenger door of the police cruiser for me.

I glance back and see Jacob's face peeking through the window upstairs. Before I can wave to him, his head disappears.

That's all I get for my family reunion, but I take solace in knowing he saw me. At least he knows I care.

I sit down at the bar, bemoaning the fact I have twenty-nine days left of my leave. What in the hell am I going to do with all that time?

"Hey, soldier, what can I get ya?"

I turn my head to answer, and the waitress bursts out in a huge smile, "Oh, my God, it's Charlie! I haven't seen you in years."

I instantly recognize Ellen, the cute brunette who was flirting with me the last day of class. I'm glad to see her, but I'm still reeling over what just happened at the house, so my answer is strained. "It's good to see you again."

She stares at me, dumbfounded. "I'm in total shock here. You've sure matured since I last saw you." She runs her hand along the sleeve of my jacket. "And, I must say, you look good in a uniform."

I chuckle. "Thanks."

She takes my order and calls out to the bartender,

"Whatever he wants, it's on me."

The bartender shakes his head. "Nothing doing, Ellen. It's on the house. Glad to have you back."

I know that voice and realize it's Arnold, the guy known for his wild parties—so tending bar makes sense. He's grown pudgier and a lot hairier since I last saw him.

"Thanks, Arnold. Appreciate it."

"So, what'll you have?"

"Jack on the rocks."

"You got it."

It feels good to be treated with respect for my service by people who are actually glad to see me. I shake my head, still in shock that my own family won't acknowledge me.

I look at Ellen again and see that flirtatious grin I remember from high school and ask, "So, tell me what you've been up to over past the seven years."

"Oh, you know, trying to stay out of trouble and make ends meet."

"No husband or kids?"

She blushes. "Haven't found the right guy yet…"

"She's too picky," Arnold calls out from the bar.

Ellen laughs.

It is a charming sound. I have been so focused on my military career, I haven't given any thought to life outside of it. But seeing Ellen again makes me question that decision.

"What are you looking for?" I ask her jokingly.

She twirls a strand of her hair when she answers. "Oh, you know, someone with a good head on his shoulders…who can sweep me off my feet."

I raise an eyebrow, seeing the invitation in her words. I ignored her invitation once, but I'm not about to again. "What time do you get off?"

She giggles excitedly and walks over to get my drink from Arnold. "Hey, what time can I cut out of here, Arn?"

"Stacey doesn't get here until four, but you can leave once she shows up."

"Thanks, Arn!"

Ellen returns to me and hands me the drink. "Will that work?"

"It's not like I have any other plans to get in the way."

"Is that because of your dad? He's been a real ass ever since you left." She suddenly gets a worried expression and covers her mouth. "I shouldn't have said that."

I shake my head in disgust. "No, you're right. He is an ass. I used to defend him, but after today…"

"What happened?"

I sigh heavily and take a drink before I answer. "Let's just say I won't be returning home."

Ellen looks worried. "Does that mean you don't have a place to stay?"

"I wasn't counting on a greeting with open arms from my father, so I've already made a reservation at Motor Inn."

"Oh, my goodness, you can't stay there! That place is swarming with bed bugs."

"Well, that's just great…"

"I've got a couch," she offers with a shy grin.

"No, I could never impose like that."

"How would it be an imposition if I make the offer?"

"People would talk," I warn her.

Ellen shrugs. "So let 'em. It'd be fun to be the center of gossip."

"I don't know…" My hesitation comes from my concern for her.

"Take her up on her offer, meathead," Arnold tells me.

"How about we start with a date and see how it goes from there?" I ask her.

"Sounds perfect, Charlie."

I spend the next few hours catching up with Arnold and Ellen. It becomes quickly apparent to me that nothing has really changed in this town, and I am grateful I left when I did. Regardless of the strain between my father and I, leaving was the best thing for me. I am light-years ahead in my career and much more experienced in life, compared to these two.

At twenty-five, I am in command of over sixty men in my platoon, and I have gained invaluable knowledge working under my commanders and the advanced training I've taken. Coming back here feels as if I've stepped back in time—and I feel out of place.

Seeking Escape

Candy

Candy,

I am glad you have accepted my offer. And yes, your picture meets my high standards.

As I said before, from this point forward, you will address me as Master.

As for you, I have chosen the pet name sextoy. Normally, I go for names such as cumwhore, but you are far too pretty for such a base name. I trust you find it acceptable.

For your first week, I have given you four simple, yet effective, tasks. On Friday, you will call me to give me a full accounting.

Task #1

Replace your current lipstick with bright red. I want men to notice those pouty lips of yours.

Task #2

I will be calling you at 8:00 PM on Wednesday. It will give us both a chance to connect a voice to

the name we see on the screen. For this phone call, I want you to wear a blindfold.

Task #3

Write my name on your thigh in permanent marker. Every time you look at yourself, I want you to be reminded of who owns you now.

Task #4

You are not allowed to wear panties the entire week.

I look forward to our conversation on Wednesday.

Master

I'm literally trembling after reading his email. While the pet name is not the romantic name I hoped for, it's far better than the other one. As far as the tasks themselves, they are simple but naughty at the same time.

I have never worn red lipstick, so that will be a big change. But the reason behind it is wicked and exciting. He wants men to look at my lips.

I am excited that I am going to get to hear his voice on Wednesday. Will it be low and dangerous like it is in my head when I read his emails?

In one email, Liege has reoriented my life. Now, all I can think about are the tasks before me and how I can accomplish them without getting caught.

It's exhilarating!

I'm feeling nervous by the time Wednesday night rolls around. Luckily, my roommate has been invited to a movie and will be out for the entire night.

Five minutes before eight, I lay the phone out in front of me and tie on my blindfold. Sitting there in the dark, waiting for his phone call, makes the minutes stretch out. When the phone finally does ring, I jump and then fumble to find it.

"Hello?"

"Hello, Master," he corrects me. His voice makes him sound like a young man about my age. I assumed he was older.

"Hello, Master," I quickly amend.

"I assume I'm talking to my sextoy."

"You are, Master."

"You have a seductive voice."

I blush, feeling butterflies in my stomach on hearing his praise. "Thank you, Master."

"How have you done with your tasks so far?"

"I'm wearing the red lipstick, your name is written on my thigh, and I'm not wearing panties, just as you asked."

"How does it make you feel?"

"It makes me feel sexy."

"Anything else?"

My heart is racing as I sit there talking to him, blindfolded. "I feel…owned."

"Good," he answers.

That simple word thrills me.

"We will keep phone calls short as I am far too busy, but I'm adding two more tasks tonight."

"Yes, Master?"

"I want to see those red lips and my name on your thigh. Send pictures of both."

"Yes, Master."

Before hanging up, he asks, "Do you enjoy being my sextoy?"

I'm surprised that I truly am, and answer softly, "Yes, Master."

I wait for my list of tasks each week, wondering what Liege has in store for me this time. It's been months, and he always manages to surprise me with new challenges.

Some tasks have been fun and exciting, like masturbating while crying out Liege's name as I come when my roommate is away.

He has also given me more challenging tasks, like buying a butt plug at a sex store and inserting it before bed so I can "train" my body while I sleep. I get wet contemplating what I'm training myself for.

Liege is *really* into orgasm denial, which means a lot of sleepless nights with me trying to deal with the unreleased sexual frustration his tasks create.

I have to admit, there was one task that scared me to death when I read it, but it turned out to be one of the most exciting. I was ordered to wear a short skirt without any panties. That was daring enough, but then I had to go out to a public place and take a picture of myself while I lifted my skirt up. It literally took hours before I had the nerve to take the picture. Oh man, it was a thrill!

Sometimes, he commands me not to wear my bra on a cold day and other days he orders me to wear dark panties under white clothing so people will notice. He likes to encourage men to have sexual thoughts about me. Even though I am always embarrassed whenever I complete those particular tasks, I must admit I've started to believe that my boyish body is actually sexy and desirable to men.

I owe that to Liege.

However, it's not all happiness and rainbows. There are some tasks I really don't care for, like when he orders me to put clothespins on my clit or nipples. That feels like a punishment to me, even though Liege says it isn't. He tells me it turns him on, knowing I'm doing something solely for his pleasure.

But the hardest part is keeping to his strict schedule. If I'm ever late for a phone call or discussion session, no matter the reason, he punishes me. I hate being punished so much I've started getting up super early to do my class assignments in the morning, instead of at night, to avoid displeasing him.

Regardless, I've been so thoroughly preoccupied by my weekly tasks, that I no longer spend my days mourning Ethan's death.

That's real progress.

My secret online relationship with Liege makes me feel more alive and confident than I ever thought would be possible after Ethan.

So, when I mention to him that spring break is coming up and he tells me I should come visit, I jump at the chance.

I understand that visiting Liege is a risky thing to do, but I really don't want to go home. There are too many memories attached to Ethan, and I can't handle pretending everything's okay with my parents. I *know* they will be watching me, just as they did when I visited them for Christmas. Worrying about every little thing I say or do—especially my dad.

I can't take that pressure.

Liege and I have had months of interaction online. I feel like I know him and can trust him.

After agreeing to an impromptu trip, I start pulling out all my clothes, wanting to pick the right outfits to impress him. Even though it's only for a few days, I pack at least a week's worth of clothes just so I have a nice variety.

My dad calls as I am stuffing my suitcase. I feel a twist in my gut, knowing he's going to be disappointed I'm not coming home. "Hey, Dad, I've got some huge projects due right after spring break and have to spend my vacation working on them. There's no point in coming home." It's only a white lie. I do have assignments I need to work on when I come back from my weekend visiting with Liege.

"But couldn't you do the work here? We haven't seen you since Christmas."

"I'll get distracted. Besides, summer vacation is just a few months away."

"Your mother and I were really counting on seeing you, C."

I know my dad is unhappy, but I can't back out of

seeing Liege now. "Give Mom a hug and know that I love you both."

"Are you really okay, C?"

I smile into the phone. "I am, Dad. I really am."

"Well…I'm glad to hear that. You're all that matters to us."

"Wish me luck on my projects," I say, wanting to get off the phone before my guilt gets the best of me.

"Luck," he says, unable to hide the disappointment in his voice.

"Love ya, Dad. Gotta go," I tell him in a light voice.

I feel bad when I hang up, but not enough to change my plans. I'm finally getting to meet Liege in person! Although he's seen pictures of me, I have never seen one of him, and I can't wait to meet my mystery Dom.

I buy cheap airline tickets using my book money for next year and fly down right after my last class. Rather than meet me at the airport, Liege has instructed me to wear a summer dress without panties and wait for him at a fancy café he frequents.

I take a taxi and try to calm my nerves the whole ride there. I feel good meeting him in a public place since this is our first time.

It makes me feel safe.

Once there, I stand before the door of the café. I suddenly feel uneasy, but I push through it when a slight breeze plays with my short dress. Being panty-less, I push the door open and step inside to escape any unwanted exposure.

My poor little heart is racing as I look around and choose a table in the corner to sit.

I wait there nervously for several minutes, wondering where Liege might be. Finally, a guy of average height and build, wearing a faded T-shirt and ripped jeans, comes up to me and sits down. He has long, stringy brown hair and a goatee. This is not quite the picture of him I had in my head. I've always imagined Liege as a successful businessman because he's said he's too busy for long phone calls.

"Hi," I say, unsure if I am supposed to call him Liege or Master in public.

He puts a finger to his lips, then slips his hand under the table. I let out a gasp when I feel his fingers between my legs.

I didn't expect this, especially in a public place, but my body is turned on by his aggressive behavior. After all, this is the same man whose name I have been crying out for months whenever I come.

Just when I get all slippery and wet, he pulls his hand away and stares at me as he licks his finger, giving a grunt of satisfaction.

I am left speechless.

When he pulls out a blindfold from his pocket and secures it over my eyes, I'm totally mesmerized, thinking how romantic and sexy that is.

Liege takes my bag and purse from me and leads me out of the café to his car. We drive in silence because he has not given me permission to speak yet. But, rather than the silence between us being intimidating, I find it arousing and mysterious. I'm left wondering what else he has planned for me.

When he parks the car, he helps me out of it and we

enter a building. I'm surprised when we climb what seems like an endless flight of stairs. At the top, he leads me down a hallway and we stop as he unlocks a door.

Once inside, Liege orders me to kneel.

I sink to the floor and wait, wondering about what's going to happen next.

I hear his footsteps as he walks around me. "You're skinnier than I expected, but I like it."

Liege takes off the blindfold and I look around his place. The apartment walls have several holes in them, and there's a spiderweb of cracks above me on the ceiling, letting me know this is a very old building.

"I wondered if you would actually come or chicken out before entering the café."

My eyes widen. "You were watching me?"

"I was. And since you are an obedient submissive…" He pulls a leather collar from his pocket and places it around my neck. "…you've earned the right to wear my collar."

I have wanted a collar, and even asked him about it once, but I am surprised that now that it's around my neck, it feels strange—not like I expected.

"Now that you're here, there is so much more I can teach you," he states with the excitement of a young boy. "But, before we do anything, I want you to call your parents."

"Why?"

"You don't want them worrying about you." He hands me my purse.

I think it's kind of sweet that he wants me to call them.

I pull out my cell phone to make the call and my dad picks up. "You okay, C?"

"Yeah." I look at Liege, who nods encouragingly. "Just overwhelmed by everything I have to get done for school."

"Take it one step at a time and you'll be fine."

"Thanks, Dad."

"You want me to go get your mother?"

"Sure, but tell her I have to keep it short. I just wanted to call before I dive back in." I laugh, adding, "Who knows? The way it looks now, you probably won't be hearing from me until summer."

I shift nervously as I wait for my mother to take the phone.

I can't believe the first thing out of her mouth is, "Cleo, you should be home. I'm worried about you."

"Why? I'm not the first college student to get buried in projects."

"But you're so fragile..."

Her words rile me up, and I immediately correct her. "I'm *not* fragile, Mom."

"You're right, sweetie." She pauses for a moment. "The truth is you're strong like your father."

I appreciate that she's trying. It means something after all we've been through. "Love you, Mom. So, don't worry about me, 'k? You take care of you, and I'll take care of me, and the three of us will meet up this summer."

"But you'll call us if you need anything?"

My dad picks the phone back up and echoes her offer, "Call us for *anything*, you hear me, C?"

"'K…" I answer, choking up a little. My dad really is the best.

Liege takes the phone and purse from me and places them in a drawer, sliding it shut. "Now, we can forget about your parents and concentrate on your training. Did you bring the cuffs?"

I nod, feeling a thrill of excitement as I get up from the floor to get them out of my suitcase.

When I look up, I see he's got a camera and is setting it up to record. When he catches me staring, he explains, "I use it for instruction. After we do a scene together, I can look over it and point out areas to improve on."

It makes sense, but I stare at the camera nervously, having never been recorded before. Once he is satisfied with the setup, he hits record and tells me to give him the leather cuffs.

I hand them to him, quivering with anticipation as he buckles a leather cuff around each of my wrists and puts my arms behind my back to clip them together.

He steps back and looks at me with a satisfied grin. "That will do fine. Now, go to the table and lie against it with your legs spread."

I move over to the small kitchen table and bend over, resting my cheek against the flat surface. Liege walks over and lifts the skirt of my dress up, exposing my bare ass.

I bite my lip, wondering what he will do.

I hear him unbuckle his belt and slide it through the loops of his jeans. "Silence," he commands.

But I let out a yelp when he slaps the belt hard against my ass.

"I said to keep silent, sextoy. There are consequences if you don't obey."

I turn to look back at him as he delivers another stroke. Tears fill my eyes. When I try to move, he rests his hand on my back. "Take your punishment like a good sub."

"But what did I do wrong?" I whimper.

He hits me with the belt again before replying. "This entire time, you have failed to address me as Master."

A cry escapes my lips when he strikes my tender ass again, the slapping sound of the leather against skin echoing in the small apartment.

"Every time you fail to be silent, I add another one."

Knowing that, I clamp my mouth shut, tears streaming down my face as he whips me with the belt several more times.

Finally, the punishment stops, and I am left trembling and in shock from his unexpected correction. He pulls me up from the table and turns me around to face him.

"There's no need for tears," he chides. "You've been punished, and I forgive you." Liege wipes away my remaining tears and smiles.

When I say nothing, he prods, "Now, what do you say…?"

In the barest of whispers, I answer, "Thank you, Master."

He leans down and gives me a chaste kiss on the lips. "That wasn't so hard, was it?"

I shake my head.

He grazes his finger over my bottom lip. "An obedient sub gets rewarded." He smiles again as he leans in to kiss me more deeply.

Somehow, those kisses rekindle my desire for him, and I am reminded of the Liege I've come to know. I look up at him hopefully when he releases me from the embrace.

"Turn around so I can look at you," he commands.

"Yes, Master."

I turn slowly, feeling his gaze on me as he assesses every angle of my body. I'm pleased when he whistles his appreciation and says, "You are a sexy little thing…"

Liege opens his arms to me and I hesitantly move to him. He enfolds me in his embrace and kisses me again, his tongue claiming my mouth as he cups my sore ass in both hands.

It is a strange thing—this unsettling mixture of attraction and fear I have for him.

It doesn't take long for me to realize that Liege has two personalities. Online, Liege has always been thoughtful and effective with his training. Most of his tasks only make me want to submit to him more.

But Liege, in person, seems immature and surprisingly inexperienced.

Rather than spending the day getting to know each other better and teaching me what he likes, Liege spends it trying out different household objects as BDSM tools. He calls them "pervertibles". It almost feels as if I'm a new toy he's experimenting with as he tests them out on me.

I don't really care for most of his pervertibles, but it's not all bad. There are a few things I enjoy very much, like the white tealights. Oh, when he drips the melting wax on my back, I shiver in pure delight. The feel of the warm wax dripping on bare skin is both ticklish and yummy, and I love it!

I also enjoy when he plays with ice cubes—trailing it over my skin and nipples, which feels deliciously cold, and then rubbing the melting ice on my clit before slipping it inside me. That alone gives me goosebumps. And then…when he slides his cock inside my cold pussy, we both experience a pleasant temperature shock. His shaft feels so red hot inside me, it's unreal, and it makes each thrust feel amazing!

Late into the night, Liege finally gives me permission to sleep, but orders me to lie on the floor beside his bed so I can remember my place.

I lie there in the dark, feeling confused as I stare up at the ceiling. Although I like the idea of being his submissive, and even love some of the things we've done today, I'm not sure I'm cut out for this lifestyle.

It feels like something vital is missing.

I'm grateful I am only here for another day. While I don't mind playing this role as his sub while I learn new things, I'm anxious to get back to school.

Despite the hard floor I fall asleep quickly, exhausted by the day's events, and wake up the following morning to find Liege staring at me from the bed.

He picks up something from his nightstand, opens it,

and hands me three Listerine breath strips. "Give your Master a morning blowjob."

I feel a little insulted that he thinks I need to freshen my breath before sucking him, but I dutifully say, "Yes, Master," before putting them in my mouth.

While they melt in my mouth, he sets up his camera. By the time he's ready, my whole mouth is tingling intensely from the minty coating left behind. Apparently, Liege feels that same intense sensation when I wrap my lips around his shaft and start sucking.

I am overcome with a sense of power as he squirms and groans with each lick and suck I give him. It's addictive, and this is the very first time since coming to visit Liege that I feel good in my role as a submissive. I like bringing him pleasure through my actions—it really excites me.

But Liege doesn't thank me for my incredible blow-job. Instead, he announces, "Today, we will test your endurance."

I feel a little uneasy about it until he produces a feather duster, and I giggle.

"Undress and lie on the bed."

I follow his command, and he ties me spread-eagle to his bed. I feel extremely vulnerable and a little sexy in this pose.

Liege proceeds to tickle me with the duster, making me giggle and laugh. But, after a while, I realize that tickling *can* be torture. When he starts using the handle of the feather duster to lightly stimulate the sensitive parts of my feet, I finally call out my safeword.

Liege stops. However, he notes the time on the clock

and makes scribbles in a notebook before he moves on to a new tool, a hairbrush.

The rest of the day, Liege logs my reaction to every pervertible he has, and even retests my response with a few he feels I called out my safeword too quickly over.

By the end of it, I feel as if I've been stretched well past my limit. When he finally tells me we're done and unbinds me, I'm so exhausted I just curl up into a ball. I'm surprised when Liege lies down on the bed beside me and wraps his arms around me.

"You have done well, my little sextoy."

I find myself coveting his simple praise.

Soon, I feel his hard cock pressing against my body as we continue to lie together. He's gentle when he takes me, still holding me in his tight embrace. Afterward, he allows me to sleep in his bed.

I wake up early that final day. To bide time while Liege finishes sleeping, I make us breakfast using the few items he has in the fridge.

Today, I head back to school to face a mountain of assignments, but I'm happy. I stare at Liege while he sleeps, wondering if our relationship will continue after this.

He wakes up before I'm done cooking and praises me for the meal I have made.

"I want you to stay longer."

I smile as I hand him the plate of food. "I'm sorry, but I can't. I have *way* too much work waiting for me."

Liege frowns.

I immediately realize I've forgotten to call him Master and quickly blurt, "Master. I meant to say Master. I'm so sorry."

His tone changes, becoming deadly serious. "I was not asking. You *will* stay longer."

My smile fades. "I can't stay…Master."

"But you will." His eyes flash with a dangerous glint.

For the first time, I feel true fear.

He finishes the rest of the breakfast in silence, but I have lost my appetite.

When Liege is done, he hands me his dish and tells me to put it in the sink. I take it from him with trepidation and go to wash it.

When I'm finished, he turns on the camera.

"Go to the table."

I shake my head and refuse to budge.

Liege grabs my arm and pulls me over to it. "You need another lesson in obedience," he states harshly. "First, a little refresher about calling me Master, then I will teach you never to say no to your Master again."

New Horizons

Charles Walker

When Stacey arrives for her shift, I escort Ellen out of the bar. "I'd offer to drive, but I don't have a car," I laugh.

Ellen smiles. "Not a problem, as long as you don't mind being seen in my Daisy."

"Daisy?"

She points to a rusty, yellow VW Bug.

I smirk. "I have no issues with flowers."

Ellen apologizes as she opens the passenger door and quickly throws everything on the seat in the back. When she turns to face me, I place my hands on her shoulders. "There's no need to apologize. You're the one doing *me* a favor."

She gazes up at me with a look of adoration. I feel the need to kiss her and I give in to that impulse. Her lips are soft and yielding. The simple kiss quickly leads to a more sensuous embrace lasting for several minutes. When I pull away, her eyes are wide and luminous.

"Wow, you can sure kiss," she says breathlessly.

"You're not so bad yourself."

"I knew I should have stopped you from leaving that day," she says with a wink.

"Well, I'm here now."

"Then get in, Charlie! Let me take you where we would have gone on a date."

I'm curious about where that would have been and get into her tiny car, buckling myself in. It's a bit cramped, but I'm not about to complain. I've gone from having no place to go to going on a date with this beautiful girl. And, based on that kiss alone, I suspect we'll be doing more before the evening is through.

Ellen takes me to the local burger joint, and I smile as she pulls into the parking lot. "I've been craving one of those greasy burgers ever since I left."

"They are as greasy as ever," she replies.

"Yeah, it seems nothing really changes around here."

"But you have," she says. "I always knew you were something special."

I laugh. "Well, it's too bad you didn't let me know before I headed out."

Ellen rolls her eyes. "Yeah, I was easily distracted back then, but I'm not anymore."

After our delicious but greasy meal, Ellen takes me to her place. I'm sad to see she's living in a rundown apartment on the west side of town. She deserves better than that.

She unlocks the door and opens it wide for me. "Ta-dah! Home sweet home."

The small place is sparsely furnished with only a

stained couch, a small kitchen table with two chairs, and an old TV set on a milk crate. I can see from the open door that she has a twin-sized bed in her bedroom.

I instantly think, *That'll make it interesting…*

"I'm sorry my place is so small, Charlie. But I have this couch you can sleep on."

"You know, it's not any smaller than where I stay on the base so, basically, it feels like home to me."

She lets out a sigh of relief. "Good. Well, I may not have much in the way of furniture, but I do have a fully stocked fridge. Would you like a beer?"

"Absolutely."

She walks over to the tiny kitchen, and I see why it's a fully stocked fridge. It's only the size of a small icebox. Ellen couldn't be living any leaner.

"So, you're waitressing now, but what are your plans for the future?" I ask, as she hands me a beer and we sit on the couch.

"I'm saving up to take an art class. I've heard from several people that I've got talent."

Art certainly isn't a moneymaker, but it'd be a better future for her than waitressing for Arnold in this stagnant town. "It's good you are pursuing it, Ellen."

She shrugs and smiles at me. "What about you?"

I give her a modest smile. "My plans haven't changed since leaving here."

"Oh, so you really are going to be a Captain?"

"In two years, if things go well."

"Wow! When you set your mind to something, you really do it, don't you?"

"This may sound crazy, but I've known it was my

calling since I was a boy. I've never questioned it."

"I don't think that's crazy at all, Charlie."

I chuckle. "Well, not everyone feels that way."

"If you're talking about your father, well, he doesn't deserve you."

I look at her tenderly. "You are kind to say that."

"I mean it, Charlie. You are a remarkable man."

The way she's looking at me invites another kiss that quickly ignites my desire for her, and there is no way to hide it.

She glances down at my erection. Rather than look shocked or embarrassed by it, she smiles and tells me, "I feel the same way, too."

I grab the back of her neck and kiss her more passionately this time, my libido spiking through the roof. I want this woman, and I want her bad.

"Maybe we should retire to the bedroom?" she suggests.

I pick her up and carry her into the bedroom without another word.

"Oh…" she giggles. "You're so strong, Charlie."

"Call me Charles," I tell her, having replaced that childish name at boot camp with Chuck. However, that was *not* what I wanted her to call me.

"Charles…" she repeats in a seductive voice.

Oh, yeah, that sounds much better.

I lay her on the tiny bed and go to unbutton my jacket.

Ellen pops off the bed, crying, "No, let me do that. I have always wanted to undress a man in uniform."

I have no complaints and watch as she slowly unbuttons the jacket, glancing at me with those bedroom eyes each time the next button is undone. After she slips off the jacket, she carefully places it on a small dresser and returns to start on the tie.

I take pleasure in seeing her enjoyment in undressing me, from unbuttoning my shirt and slipping off my shoes and socks, to unbuckling my belt and unzipping my trousers. I stand before her in my briefs, sporting a major hard-on.

She falls to her knees and smiles up at me. "That is as much fun as I thought it would be, but this…" She looks at my crotch. "…this will be my favorite part."

I hold my breath as she pulls down my briefs.

Ellen stares at me hungrily. "Oh, yes, that's nice."

Without my having to ask, she takes pity on my cock and grasps it in her hand before placing her lips on the head of my shaft. I release the air in my lungs and groan as she goes down on my cock.

Oh hell…

Even though she doesn't go deep, her repeated bobbing drives me wild. I have to stop her several times to prevent myself from coming to soon. When I can't take any more, I help her up and begin undressing her.

Her skin is soft, and those breasts are sweet and perky.

I must taste them.

I lift her small frame and take a liberal taste of one of her nipples. Her soft moan shoots a current of electricity straight to my groin. I move to the other nipple, sucking harder.

I want her. I want all of her.

She clings to me with her legs around my waist as I walk to the nearest wall and push her up against it.

I *need* this girl, and I release my pent-up desire by sucking, licking, and biting her skin. I could eat her up, she tastes so good to me.

Ellen cries out in passion, inviting the attention.

Her cries incite my baser instincts, and I take her to the bed, throwing her on it. I move between her legs, needing to bury myself deep inside her. Her pussy is wet and ready, but I stop myself just in time.

Through gritted teeth, I tell her, "I have a condom in my bag. Let me get it."

"Don't bother. I have one in the top drawer," she answers, pointing to her dresser. I lean over to pull the drawer out and retrieve it. I rip at the wrapper and slip the rubber over my cock. I move back into position, and ask before I bury myself deep inside her, "Do you like it rough?"

"Oh, God, yes!" she cries.

Her answer is music to my ears because I want her too much to be gentle. I spread her legs wide and push my cock into her wet pussy in one solid stroke. Ellen cries out lustfully, begging for more.

I love the sound of her passionate screams and give it to her harder and deeper. I revel in her warm pussy squeezing my needy cock. But it isn't enough.

I want it deeper, so I pull out and flip her around.

"On your hands and knees," I growl huskily.

She immediately assumes the position, and I sink my shaft back into her, giving her the pounding of her life. I stop a few times to feel her pussy milk my cock with her orgasms. However, it feels too good and I finally give in to the urge to release myself.

All reason leaves me as the buildup reaches the edge of my endurance. I groan loudly as I come hard, thrusting as deep as I can. I stop, keeping my shaft buried inside her, and sigh in satisfaction as she comes around my cock one last time.

Afterward, I hold her in my arms on her impossibly small bed, while we catch our breaths.

"You…" she says in a voice hoarse from good sex, "…you are a fucking machine!"

"Thanks."

"No, I'm serious, Charles. I've never experienced anything like you before."

"You date a lot?"

She blushes. "Not much, because nobody meets my standards."

"So, Arnold wasn't kidding, huh?"

"Do you mind if I'm totally honest with you?"

"I wouldn't want it any other way."

Ellen gives me a shy smile when she confesses, "I compare them all to you, Charles."

"But you hardly knew me in high school."

"Not true. I followed everything you did—all your track meets, all those scholastic competitions. I kept up on all of it."

"Why didn't you ever let me know?"

"Are you kidding? You're so smart, and handsome, and…" She moves back a little to look me over. I am totally expecting to hear her say, "A great fuck." Instead, she surprises me. "You're ambitious, Charles. I've never met anyone like you."

"But that doesn't explain why you kept dating other guys if you were interested in me."

She shrugs. "What would a girl like me have to offer you?"

I run my finger over her lips. "You have that beautiful smile." My hands move down to her breasts. "And these delicious breasts." I then place my hand over her heart. "As well as a generous heart. That's more than enough for any man."

Ellen looks as if she's about to cry. "Damn it, Charles. That's not fair."

I chuckle. "What's not fair?"

"Now I love you even more."

I pull her onto me, pressing her small body against mine, and kiss her on the head.

After a few moments, she says, "Charles."

"Yes, Ellen?"

"Is that…?"

"Yes, it is."

"I've never had a guy get hard again that fast."

"My cock likes you. So, are you ready for round two?"

By the end of my leave, I find myself reluctant to go. Ellen is too important for me to treat this like a casual hookup.

I'm in love with the girl.

I debate with myself what to do, but I can only see one solution if I want to keep her in my life without compromising my career.

I enter the bar, dressed in my Army service uniform, and walk straight up to her. She looks distraught. "It's not time yet, is it? Don't you have a few more days?"

"I do," I answer, holding my arm out to her. "Would you care to come with me?"

She shakes her head, smiling. "What's this about? I still have five hours on my shift."

I nod to Arnold. "I okayed it with the boss."

She looks over to him and he nods. Wrapping her arm around mine, she giggles. "I must be dreaming. A handsome man in uniform is asking me to leave work on a date? Pinch me now."

I lead her out and take pleasure in her squeal. "A limo? Oh my… I really *am* dreaming."

I open the door for her. "Your chariot awaits."

"Oh, Charles, I can't believe this," she gushes as she gets inside.

I have already instructed the driver where to go. I want to share a special place with her. One that no one else knows about, except my brother, Jacob.

The ride takes nearly forty-five minutes from the bar. That whole time, Ellen is bouncing from seat to seat, wanting to take it all in. "It's so big!"

"That's what she said."

Ellen looks at me and then bursts out laughing, moving back over to me to give me a hug and a kiss. "You're my dream come true, Charles Walker."

I take her hand and kiss it, anxious to reach our destination.

The driver takes us up to the summit of the hilltop and pulls to the side of the road. I exit the vehicle and help her out. "This is the place I used to go to as a kid," I explain.

"All the way up here?"

"Yeah, it made for a challenging bicycle ride as a kid, but I liked the view."

"It is impressive," she agrees, looking at our town and the great expanse of plains beyond it.

"Seeing my world from this view opened my mind to the possibility of life beyond this place, beyond my father's expectations. Once I was set free of those boundaries, I realized I could dream as big as I wanted. It was when I allowed myself to imagine a future without limits, that I had my vision. This exact spot," I point to the ground, "is where I knew I was meant to be part of the Army."

Ellen hugs herself against me. "You were extraordinary, even as a kid."

"I say all this, so you can understand how important my future plans are."

"I know, Charles."

"However, coming back here made me realize I've left out an important part of my life."

She looks up into my eyes. "What's that?"

"You." I pull her to me and whisper in her ear before I kiss her deeply. "I love you, Ellen." I feel her tremble in my arms.

"Oh, Charles, you've made me so happy!"

"I don't want to leave you behind, but I need to finish what I've started. Would you be willing to wait for me? I'll come back whenever I can take leave. It'll take longer to make Captain, but it's worth the sacrifice."

"Time away from you will be hard," she pouts.

"It will be but, if you're willing to wait for me, I'll make it worth your while."

Her lips begin to tremble when I get down on one knee and pull out the ring in my pocket. "Ellen, will you marry me?"

She bounces up and down on her toes. "Charles, I can't believe this!"

I cock my head, smiling up at her while I wait patiently for her answer.

"Yes, of course," she says, giggling excitedly. "Of course, I will!"

I pick her up and twirl her in the air several times, ecstatic she's agreed to be my wife. When I set her back down on the ground, I share my plans with her.

"I will do what I can to take care of you while we're apart."

She grins, shaking her head. "What do you mean, Charles?"

"I'm going to get you into a better apartment and get you some real furniture. I'll even help pay for that art class you talked about."

"Oh, my goodness! You'd do that for me? You're too much!"

I kiss her again. "I want my fiancé well cared for."

"I love hearing you call me that," she coos. "I love you, Charles."

I wrap my arms around her. "I love you, too." It

feels so good to say those words and know they are returned.

I look down at my hometown below us and feel complete. My future is out there, but a part of that future will tie me to my past when I marry Ellen.

Making the most of the last few days we have together, I help Ellen pick out new furniture and sign a contract for a more spacious apartment on the west side of town.

As she's admiring her new kitchen and full-sized fridge, I tell her, "I'll send you money monthly to help with your rent and cover costs."

"Thank you, Charles, but I feel bad taking money."

"Nonsense. I want to know you're taken care of."

"You're too good to me."

I take her hand and press it to my lips. "I plan to spoil you on my return."

Ellen sighs as I embrace her. "I hate that you are leaving."

I hold her tight, feeling the loss already. "I just need you to keep your sights on the future. I'll be back every six months, if I can. It might feel like forever, but when you know you're heading toward something you want, it makes it easier."

"Well, I definitely want you," she purrs, giving me a playful nip. "But you have to promise me you'll stay away from the girls. *No one* touches my handsome military man."

"Of course." I play with the engagement ring on her finger. "You and I get to enjoy the challenge of a celibate life, but we can make up for it every time I return."

"Then I guess we won't be leaving the bedroom at all," she laughs.

I steal a kiss from her before grabbing a letter from my bag. "I do have a favor to ask."

"Anything, Charles."

"Could you give this to Jacob? I'm not sure he's gotten any of my letters."

She presses it against her chest. "It would be my honor."

"I need Jacob to know I've been saving up for his college. If he ends up not wanting to go to the Air Force Academy, I want him to know he has money for traditional college."

Tears fill her eyes. "Oh, that's so sweet of you."

I shrug. "Jacob should know that Father's plan for his life doesn't have to be his."

Ellen throws her arms around me. "You just make me love you more."

I raise an eyebrow. "You want to show me how much?"

"Yes, I do, Lieutenant Walker…"

I lead her to the bigger bed I've purchased and ask Ellen to do a striptease for me. I'm mesmerized by her flirtatious smile as she undresses before me.

I feel good about my decision. Taking on Ellen's expenses on top of Jacob's schooling is not a hardship for me. I'm only one man, and this investment ensures a strong future for both my career and personal life.

An Invitation

Candy

My life now centers around Liege.

He never leaves the apartment, working from home on his computer and ordering his groceries online. He's locked my purse and phone in his desk but tells me I can get them back when he's satisfied with my training.

I spend my days trying to fulfill his every need and, when I fail, I am punished for it.

Soon, his voice is the only one I hear in my head.

It's shocking how, in the span of a few weeks, I've gone from being a girl looking for a kinky escape to feeling like a slave.

Liege slams his fists on his desk and gets up from his computer, growling irritably, "I have to go out, but you're staying here."

I can't believe he is leaving, and my heart begins racing as he buckles the cuffs onto my wrists and secures them to the bed. Not taking chances, he gags me before heading out.

As soon as I hear the distinctive whine of his car engine starting to fade down the street, I struggle against the cuffs. They fit loosely when I bought them, and I've lost weight in the weeks since.

After several minutes of concentrated effort, I wrestle one hand out. I feel positively giddy as I unbuckle my other wrist and rip off the gag.

I go straight for the computer desk.

I pull hard on the drawer, hoping to break the internal lock with my bare hands, but I have no luck. So I start searching his desk, hoping to find the key. In my search, I come across a book with a title that catches my attention.

Bow at My Feet: A Master's Tale of Online Training

I open it up and feel a cold chill run down my spine as I skim the pages. It is an autobiography about a Dom who seeks out a girl online and trains her to be his submissive. The author has laid it all out in his book, including the tasks he gives her and the psychological reasoning behind each one.

What is simply a chronicle about one man's experience, Liege has been treating like a manual, copying *everything* this man does to the letter. It suddenly makes sense why the person I knew online was not the person I met when I came here.

Liege lied about everything. He is not even a Dom!

After several sweeps of the desk fail to produce the key, I go to the kitchen and grab the hammer out of a junk drawer. I go back to the desk and start whacking at it. I feel a surge of hope when the metal starts to bend. I pull on it again and the drawer opens a crack. I force my fingers inside and start pulling for all I am worth.

I'm so close…

I grab the hammer again and hit it even harder. I wrench the drawer open enough to reach inside, and I feel a sense of exhilaration when I touch my purse. I tug on it, but the opening is not quite big enough, so I start hammering at it again.

My heart skips a beat when the hammer stops mid-strike and is wrenched from my hands. I look up to see Liege and panic. Sprinting toward the door, I cry out when I find it locked and start pounding on it in desperation.

Dread fills my heart when I turn around to see Liege approaching me with the hammer clutched in his hand.

I start screaming.

To my relief, Liege throws the hammer to the side, but backhands me hard across the face, ordering me to shut up—but I refuse.

He covers my mouth with one hand while choking me with the other. I bite the fleshy part of his palm and he immediately uncovers my mouth, using both hands to choke me instead.

I see flashing lights as my vision starts to blur.

I suddenly can breathe again when Liege lets go of my throat and picks me up to throw me face-first on the bed. With his knee digging into my back, Liege ties the gag back on and secures the cuffs behind my back.

I lie there, whimpering, waiting for the pain of his belt, but nothing happens.

I'm left there, bound and helpless, listening to him putting the hammer back in the drawer before quietly straightening his desk as if nothing is wrong.

It feels like the calm before the storm.

Finally, Liege speaks, his tone unsettlingly serene. "I told you that you would get your things back when you were properly trained."

He pauses for a moment before continuing.

"Did you think there would be no consequences for disobeying me?"

I whimper. I was so close…

"If my car hadn't broken down, I wouldn't have been here to stop you from making the biggest mistake of your life." He walks over and fists my hair, pulling my head back to look at him. "You're lucky I'm a good Master."

I pant with fear, waiting to find out my punishment.

"You *must* pay for destroying my desk. Can you guess how you're going to do that?"

I shake my head slowly.

Liege smiles as he pulls out a permanent marker and shows it to me before lifting my skirt and pulling off my panties. Instead of the sting of a belt, I feel the cool ink of the marker as he writes a word on each of my buttocks. Afterward, he chuckles with satisfaction.

"You have earned a new name. It's time to show it off."

As Liege undoes my bindings, he tells me, "I'm giving you *one* chance. You either prove you can obey or I will send your parents your sex tapes. You know, that one where you deepthroat my cock while you look at me with those sexy eyes. Or the one where you call me 'Daddy' and beg me to fuck you in the ass. You took it pretty deep in that one, I might add. And those are just the tame ones, aren't they?"

I feel like I have been hit in the gut.

"I wonder," he continues with a smile, "what Mommy and Daddy would say if they found out their little girl has been lying to them. That instead of coming home for spring break, she chose to come here and do depraved things with me?"

My stomach turns, horrified at the thought of them seeing the tapes. My parents could never live it down—especially my mother. They can never know what I've done!

"So, you will take your punishment without complaint. Do you understand?"

I nod my head, defeated.

Liege removes the gag from my mouth and orders me to freshen up.

"Make yourself pretty for me."

With shaking hands, I brush my hair and put on the lipstick he likes. When he looks me over, he seems pleased and hands me my shoes.

My heart quickens as I slip into the flip-flops, not really believing I'm about to leave this apartment. But when I make the mistake of grabbing for my panties, he clears his throat in warning.

I quickly set them down and look at him fearfully. To my relief, he opens the door and orders me to follow him. Liege puts his arm around me, as if in a romantic embrace, as we walk out of the building.

I haven't been outside in weeks and feel lightheaded as I take in the fresh air and feel the warmth of the sun on my skin. It feels like it's been forever.

Liege walks us to the train station with his arm still around me. I try to make eye contact with the other commuters, hoping someone will see something's wrong, but everyone is staring at their phones.

We get onto the train together, and Liege pushes me toward an empty seat. I sit down, trying not to cry, wondering what he wants me to do.

Once the train starts moving, he leans down and tells me in a low voice, "You are going to show off your new name to everyone. Turn around and lift up your dress."

I shake my head.

His eyes flash with anger. "Do *not* defy me."

I close my eyes, knowing I have to, but I can't.

He snarls under his breath, "I'm not asking."

I lower my head as a tear travels down my cheek.

When I don't obey, he warns, "You understand there will be consequences…"

I shudder, knowing what it will do to my family. My mother might not recover from the shock. I look up at him pleadingly. "I'm sorry."

Liege turns away. "Apologies mean nothing."

More tears fall. I know I will pay for defying him, but I can't do this—I won't let him do this to me.

"You have one more chance to make this right," he

tells me.

I glance at the train full of people, my bottom lip trembling as I whisper, "I can't."

A pleasant voice breaks the terrible silence that follows.

"Sir, may I speak with her?"

"Who the hell are you?" Liege snaps.

The young woman lowers her gaze and answers in a pleasant voice, "I'm no one, sir. But I have a humble suggestion for your girlfriend with the lovely collar."

Liege snorts, puffing his chest out as he looks her up and down. "Fine, you may speak."

The woman kneels beside me and smiles. "Hi, my name is Brie. What's yours?"

I look at Liege fearfully for permission to speak before I answer. "Candy. My name is Candy."

Her eyes sparkle when she tells me, "That's a good name. You look perfectly delicious."

This girl is like a ray of light in the darkness, and I find myself smiling. I watch as she looks in her purse and holds out a business card to me. "May I humbly suggest this course? It's changed my life."

Before I can take it, Liege grabs it. "What's this?"

He laughs harshly. "Yes, this is *exactly* what you need," he says, giving me the card.

I look down at it and see the words:

The Submissive Training Center
Twenty-five years of Excellence

I feel the woman's hand on my knee. "Trust me.

This will change your life for the better."

I feel my spirits lift when I look into her honey-colored eyes.

By the way he keeps looking her over, it is obvious Liege is quite taken by the elegant woman. I gasp in shock when he grabs her chin and tells her, "You are a lovely thing. Come with us so I can see what you've learned at this Center of yours."

The woman pulls away and returns her gaze to the floor while she answers him in a respectful tone, "I'm sorry, sir, but I cannot."

Liege does not like the woman's answer and glares at her, demanding, "Why?"

The woman lovingly caresses the collar she wears around her neck and answers, "Only my Sir commands me."

Liege laughs unkindly. "Loyal, are you?" He then turns to me and says, "You could learn a lot from this one. Maybe I'll let you take the class. You need it because, truth be told, you suck."

The woman ignores his insult targeted at me and responds instead with a respectful, "Thank you, sir," before walking back gracefully to her seat.

I stare at her in awe. She is like an angel in the darkness.

That short exchange has changed Liege. I can feel his anger dissipating as he stares at the beautiful submissive. He wants her, and that desire just might save me.

When we return to his apartment, Liege tells me to stand in the corner while he decides my fate.

He starts pacing back and forth. "Why can't you be like her?" he complains.

"I want to be," I tell him in earnest.

Liege walks over and looks at me, before stating in disgust, "But you're not her. You could never be like her."

He starts pacing the floor again. "Oh, God, to be able to fuck something like that every night…"

I want to laugh. That woman would never submit to someone as pathetic as Liege.

"Give me the card," he demands.

I have held it in my hand ever since she gave it to me like it is a ward of protection, and I am reluctant to give it to him, but I do.

He looks at the business card and glances at me, before going to the computer.

Liege types in the website address printed on it and spends the next few hours poring over the sensual photos of submissives in training. I watch in the corner, grateful that he seems to have forgotten my punishment—for now.

Several days later, a large envelope arrives. Liege rips it open and smiles at me. "You will write down everything I say."

"Of course, Master," I immediately answer, walking over to the kitchen table. I look down at the papers he pushes in front of me and see it's an application for the Submissive Training Center.

My heart skips a beat and I stare at it in disbelief.

"How?"

"I emailed them as you. Now you'll have no excuse for being a shitty sub."

I spend the next hour writing down Liege's answers to the long list of questions on the application. Afterward, he hands me a tiny red plastic stick and tells me to play with myself while he records me.

I take it from him but have no idea what to do and freeze up when he starts recording. When I fail to do an adequate job, Liege insists on directing me through it as he records me. By the time he is finished, he's so thrilled with the video that he watches it several times.

Afterward, he uploads it to a memory stick and throws it into the envelope, along with all of the paperwork. When he sends off the packet, he warns me, "You better make it in or Mommy dearest is about to get the shock of her life."

I silently pray I will be accepted, not only to protect my parents, but for myself. The fact is, I want to be like that woman on the train. She looked so confident and beautiful, and I will never forget the way she lovingly caressed her collar.

I want to know that kind of devotion…

I can tell that something big is up when a large box is left at the door. Liege brings it in with an excited look on his face. He begins pacing as he reads the attached letter.

"Hell, yeah!" he shouts, slapping the letter with the back of his hand several times, before pushing it in my face so I can read it.

Dear Miss Cox,

It is my pleasure to inform you that you have qualified for a full scholarship to the Submissive Training Center. Your entry was notable, and we believe the opportunity provided by our school will be of great benefit to you, now and in the future.

As stated in an earlier email, you will begin the course immediately. The first class begins Monday at 7:00 PM. You must be prompt and prepared to learn.

A school uniform has been provided for you.

This is a six-week course designed to increase your knowledge of the unique dynamics behind a D/s relationship and to challenge your growth as a submissive beyond what you know now. We expect much from you, but we promise the expert training you receive will expand your horizons significantly.

Yours Truly,
Headmaster Coen

I feel goosebumps as I read the letter. It feels as if Headmaster Coen has written it specifically to me.

Liege tears open the box and starts pulling out the contents. My school uniform consists of a purple satin corset, black miniskirt, a red thong, a pair of impossibly tall heels, and crotchless pantyhose with sexy seams up the back. Also included are a black trench coat and an elaborate makeup kit with instructions.

He insists I put my uniform on, including the

makeup. Once I'm all done up, he stares at me with a critical eye and complains, "But you're nothing like her."

I peek at myself in the mirror and think, *Maybe someday I will be...*

Dear John

Captain

I return to service a new man, charged up after an extremely productive leave. I'm determined to stay in constant communication with Ellen through letters and phone calls, so we don't lose the connection we have with each other.

I have to say, seeing that first letter waiting for me seriously makes my day.

Dearest Charles,

You have only been gone a little more than a week, and yet it feels like forever to me. I miss you so much!

I wanted to make you proud, so I enrolled in my class as soon as your money came. Wish me luck! It starts next month, and I'm a little nervous about it, but excited too.

I have to pinch myself to believe all this is

real.

You are truly my knight in shining armor.

Since you're paying for my class, the next time I see you, I promise to paint your portrait as my way of saying thank you. Then, when I become a famous artist, you can sell it for big bucks and I'll have paid you back! Ha-ha.

Seriously, I can't thank you enough.

Oh, you'll be happy to hear I gave your mom the letter to Jacob. We bumped into each other at the grocery store, so it worked out perfectly. She seemed interested in hearing how you were doing but was surprised when I told her we're engaged.

By the way, I'm loving this new apartment, Charles! It's so nice that I invited a few friends over for a house warming party and they couldn't stop going on about how lucky I am. And I agree, I am lucky! I feel like my whole life has changed because of you.

By the way, did I tell you I miss you?

Confession time. I stare at your picture at night, but it drives me crazy. Oh, how I miss that sexy body, soldier!

Love you, Charles.

My man.

My everything.

Hugs, kisses, and naughty bits,
Ellen

The end of her letter has me grinning. That girl is the perfect combination of sexy and sweet.

I actually tear up as I reread the part about Ellen's encounter with my mother. There's so little about her or what was said between them. I would have preferred Ellen giving the letter directly to my little brother, but my mother is the next best choice. At least now my family knows of my plans to marry.

I fold the letter up and slip it back in its envelope. I suspect this forced separation will be difficult for Ellen. However, I am equally confident that the sacrifice will be worth it.

I had no idea what I was missing until now. What a fool I was not to come home sooner…

My expertise in searching out and destroying enemy reserves has garnered the attention of senior officers, and I have been entrusted with training several new men slotted for advancement.

One of them is a man of small stature at only five-six, but this kid's a real gun bunny. In the heat of battle this cannoneer's enthusiasm and accuracy hitting targets stands out, as does his willingness to help the other crews.

I see Gallant's strength and potential, but my platoon only sees his height, and that is beginning to affect his performance and theirs, so I take him aside.

"Gallant, I need to speak with you."

"Of course, Lieutenant Walker."

He stops what he is doing and catches up with me as I walk away from the others. "This may be uncomfortable for you to hear," I begin.

"Yes, Lieutenant Walker," he answers, looking at me with concern.

"You're an excellent cannoneer. One of the best I've seen. However, I'm starting to notice a change."

He furrows his brow. "How so?"

"The other men aren't treating you with the respect your skill and experience demands."

He looks toward the ground, nodding thoughtfully. "It *is* becoming a problem."

I appreciate that he recognizes the issue rather than denying it. "What do you plan to do?"

"I've been contemplating it for weeks now—obviously without success. I get that I'm short, but that has no bearing on my abilities in the field."

"Exactly," I agree.

He stops walking and turns to face me. "Do you have any suggestions, Lieutenant?"

"You have the talent and drive as a leader, but you lack one vital component."

He lowers his eyes for a moment but returns his gaze to mine, wanting to face the truth. "What is it, Lieutenant?"

"Confidence."

Gallant frowns. "But I know I'm capable. I've never doubted that—not for a second."

"You are capable," I agree, "but you think like a lesser man."

Gallant takes in a long breath, struggling not to respond.

I continue, undeterred. "There are men who have the skills, but lack confidence on the battlefield. The only thing that can break that is time and experience. You, however, have the ability to overcome your issue now."

"How do I do that?"

"Change your thinking."

"In what way?" he asks, clearly interested.

We continue walking as I explain, "You know your strengths and what you bring to your team, but you're allowing the men to define you."

He nods his head.

"Only you have the power to change that."

"How?"

"Forget your stature, rather than trying to compensate for it. It's a mistake many men make. Humans respond to confidence because it equates to strength and leadership. If my men believe in you, looks won't have any impact. Be confident in what you bring to the table, Gallant," I say, putting my hand on his shoulder, "and they will respond instinctively. Understand, it's not something that you work at. It's something you believe without question."

Gallant nods as he takes in my words. After a few moments, he meets my gaze again. I can already see a change in him. I turn around to head back. "It's an honor to have you on my team, Private First Class."

"The honor is mine, Lieutenant Walker."

Gallant isn't the only notable addition. My old Battle Buddy has also joined the team.

"Never thought we'd meet like this, Warrant Officer Bell."

Grapes gives me a salute, then shakes my hand. "Look at you, going all First Lieutenant on me, Walker."

"Excuse me. That's First Lieutenant Walker to you."

"Yes, sir!" he replies overenthusiastically.

I answer in my best impression of our old Drill Sergeant "Did I give you permission to call me *sir*?" We both chuckle, remembering our basic training days.

"How close are you to becoming Captain?" he asks.

"Give me a couple of years."

"Pretty impressive considering you started right out of high school."

"It's called fortitude and perseverance."

He rolls his eyes good-naturedly. "Mixed with a little insanity."

I chuckle. "How about you? Are you planning to head up the ranks?"

"I'm still debating. As Warrant Officer, I get to do what I love, and I don't have to take a pay cut as a Second Lieutenant."

I nod. "I can respect your reasoning."

"So, you get any letters from home these days?" he asks in a teasing tone.

"I do, in fact." I pull out my wallet and show him a picture of Ellen. "This is my fiancé. We're set to marry in two years."

"How did an ugly cuss like you score a hot chick?"

"I'm a lucky bastard. What can I say?"

He looks at her picture more closely and *tsks*. "She's a looker, but I'd rather bang more pussy than commit to a single woman."

"It's all about the quality, not the quantity."

"Oh, it's quality snatch we're talking here, buddy. Nothing but the best for this dick."

"Dick is right," I agree, laughing at him. "What about you? Any letters from home?"

"Nah," he snarls. "Nothing's changed on that front, and I'll never go back home until I'm in a body bag."

I find it difficult to laugh at that. "Sorry to hear it, man."

"What about your father? Still gunning for the Ass of the Year award?"

I chuckle, trying to hide my resentment. "Yeah, some things never change."

"Hey, what about your little brother? You still write the kid?"

"Every damn Tuesday. I was hoping to see him when I went home, but my father called the police. I have a college fund waiting for him, if he decides he doesn't want to go to the Air Force Academy."

Grapes looks at me thoughtfully. "You're a good guy, BS."

I slap him on the back and laugh. "Ah, go fuck yourself."

"No, that's you, Mr. Commitment. Me? I'll take a wet pussy over a hand job any day."

Yeah, it's good to have the prick back in my life.

Our unit has been deployed overseas to assist in the training of foreign troops as part of the Camp David Peace Accord. It's far from home and makes the separation from Ellen more pronounced as I wait to hear from her. Her letters have been coming less frequently ever since I left on this mission.

When I see I've finally gotten one, I feel a sense of relief. Ellen doesn't realize it, but her letters hold even more importance to me now that I'm far from home.

I keep it tucked in my chest pocket and don't pull it out until I am alone that night. I rip open the envelope and pull out a letter that's three pages long. At least she's making up for lost time.

Dear Charles,

I know it's been so long since I have written.

But I wanted to let you know I've enrolled in several more art classes at the studio. Diego tells me that my work is unique and additional classes will help me truly unleash my passion on the canvas.

He also says that talent like mine is rare and needs to be channeled. Diego is a genius, Charles, a true genius. The fact he feels that way about my work really means something.

I've learned so much from him, not only about art, but also about myself. That is the reason I am writing you this letter.

Please know, I never meant for this to happen...

I put the letter down, knowing what this is.

I walk away, grabbing a cigarette—a habit I've picked up since coming down here. Taking a couple of drags, I stare at the letter.

She's fucking the art teacher.

I laugh out loud, knowing I paid for the class so we would have a future together and now she is fucking the asshole.

I put out the butt and field strip the cigarette, stuffing the filter in my pocket before grabbing another cigarette and lighting up.

Picking up the letter again, I skim through the rest of it. After a lengthy explanation, detailing how Diego had a run of bad luck and needed a place to stay, and peppering her letter with assurances that she still loves me as a friend, Ellen finally cuts to the chase by breaking off the engagement, but asking if she can keep the ring.

I scribble down my response on a piece of paper.

Heard.

Return my ring.

I stick it in an envelope and address it, seething with

anger. What the hell happened to loyalty?

It's one thing for Ellen to have fallen for another guy, but to ask him to live with her while still wearing my ring and accepting my financial support...

I immediately fill out the paperwork to suspend further payments to her.

There is a feeling of justice knowing she will struggle without my money, but I am also overwhelmed by a profound sense of loss. I take out my photo and stare at her smiling face. I thought I had found the one.

My future.

Knowing I was wrong hurts like fucking hell.

It seems I will never know the love of family or a good woman. The only people I can trust are my own men—they are my family now.

When the ring finally shows up, weeks later, I give it to a private. Rumor has it he's in love with a girl back home and is saving up for a ring so he can propose to her.

I hope to hell that the kid has better luck than I.

With my life in shambles, I return to my relentless quest to become Captain of a battery. *Nothing* is going to stand in the way of me realizing that dream.

Rescue

Candy

Liege can't wait for me to begin my first day of training and drives me there a half hour before class starts. He's chomping at the bit once we arrive and tells me, "I want you to show me everything you learn tonight as soon as we get home."

"Yes, Master."

His excitement suddenly dissolves, and he stares at me with a troubled expression. "These Dominants aren't going to be forgiving like I am, so you damn well better do everything they say. Don't you dare disappoint them. You hear me? If you get kicked out of this program…" He shakes his head.

I blurt out, "I will do everything they say, Master."

"And in case you have any ideas about leaving me…" He pulls out one of the tapes. "I won't hesitate to share your sex tapes with the world, starting with good ol' Mom and Dad."

I burn with shame and lower my head, mumbling. "I

won't say anything."

"See that you don't, or I promise there's going to be hell to pay." Liege grabs my black trench coat from the back of the car and orders me to put it on.

I stare down at the gorgeous corset I'm wearing and feel a surge of confidence. I love my school uniform and can't wait to see what real Doms are like. I expect they will be intimidating, but I will do whatever it takes to stay in their good graces. The fact that I can be free of Liege every evening is worth whatever I'm asked to do.

Liege grasps my arm in a possessive hold and heads into the building which, surprisingly, looks like a business college. He goes directly to the reception desk and explains who he is to the woman, adding, "This is my submissive, she has class tonight."

The woman graces me with a warm smile. "Ah, yes, Miss Cox. The Training Center is one floor down. Just take the elevator to your right."

Liege starts to lead me there, but she stops him. "I'm sorry, but only students are allowed on the lower level."

He turns to face her, frowning.

She responds with a pleasant smile. "Class ends promptly at twelve. You can return to pick her up then."

"I want to meet the trainers," Liege demands.

She hands him a piece of paper. "Please write down your request and I will make sure the Headmaster sees it."

"Are you telling me I can't meet them now?"

"That's correct. They are busy preparing for the first session. However, I promise to give this to Headmaster Coen before class ends tonight."

Liege growls. "I don't like handing my sub over to people I don't know."

"Your concern is understandable, but I assure you that the staff at the Submissive Training Center are the best of the best, which is why admission to the course is so difficult to get."

"I don't like this," he huffs, looking at me.

I am suddenly afraid he will change his mind and take me back to his apartment.

"I suggest you note that on your request," the receptionist replies. "We are always seeking to improve the school for our clients."

Liege scribbles his complaint and folds it in half before handing it back to her.

"Thank you, Mr…?" She looks at him, waiting for an answer.

He gives her a smirk and replies, "You can call me Master."

"I'm sorry. I cannot," she responds without blinking.

Liege shrugs. "It was worth a shot. You're a little old for me, but I like your rack."

The receptionist ignores him and turns to face me, handing me a business card. "My name is Rachael and this is my business card. If you have any questions after class tonight, please call. I'm always happy to help."

Liege snatches it from me and slips it into his own pocket, looking at her suggestively. "I'll keep that in mind, Rachael."

To my relief, Liege turns and walks out the door, not even bothering to look back.

"Miss Cox, please proceed to class," Rachael encourages me. "Enjoy your first day."

I head toward the elevator doors, smiling to myself. The artful way she handled Liege means I get to stay. I press the button with an inner sigh of relief.

While I wait for the elevator, a man comes up and stands beside me. When I walk into it, I give him a sideways glance. He's taller than me, with a slim build and pale skin. The man seems to feel my stare and turns his head. His dark eyes instantly capture my attention and I find I can't look away.

"Your name?" he asks in a smooth voice.

"Candy. Candy Cox."

"Ah, Miss Cox." He holds out his hand. "You are the recipient of our scholarship. It is a pleasure to meet you in person. I'm Marquis Gray."

I feel a jolt go through me when he stares into my eyes. It seems like he is looking straight into my soul and I shiver unconsciously.

"I trust you will find tonight's class enlightening," he tells me.

I simply nod, completely tongue-tied.

When the doors open, he surprises me by escorting me to the class. "Mr. Gallant, we have a student who has come early tonight. Is it okay if she remains here, or would you prefer she go to the commons to wait?"

A smaller man with silver highlights in his hair and a sinewy frame walks over to us. Mr. Gallant's smile is warm and compassionate. "You are welcome to choose a desk and wait for the others to arrive, Miss Cox."

Although the man is not that much taller than I am, he has a commanding voice and demeanor that gives me butterflies. "Thank you, Mr. Gallant."

I look over at Marquis Gray and blush—he's just so intense. "Thank you for showing me to class, Mr. Gray."

"You can call me Marquis."

"Thank you, Marquis."

He nods, looking at me thoughtfully. "I expect great things from you, Miss Cox."

I tremble as he leaves, hoping desperately I don't disappoint him.

During class with Mr. Gallant, I am shocked to learn that submissives maintain control and are allowed to voice preferences and set limits.

"A submissive offers her submission to a Dominant. It is a gift that should be treasured."

My heart skips a beat.

Mr. Gallant also explains the different types of subs and tells us that even with a full-time Master, although the sub may set very few limitations on the Dominant, the submissive still has control—she just chooses not to use it.

I've never understood how much power a submissive really has until now, and I realize it is an important piece missing in my relationship with Liege.

Mr. Gallant explains to our class, "A submissive finds pleasure in serving the needs and desires of another. When that is coupled with a Dominant who seeks to guide and care for the submissive, it makes for a harmonious partnership."

I feel my heart starting to beat faster. What he is saying makes sense to my soul. My desire to serve is not wrong, but the man I've chosen most definitely is. I touch the collar around my neck.

It feels like a noose now.

We head off to class where I meet Marquis Gray again, along with three other trainers. Headmaster Coen, who is extremely muscular and seems to be very serious when it comes to following instructions and rules. Master Anderson, who is very tall and deliciously well built. He comes off a little strict but, every now and then, I see a twinkle in his eye that makes me think there is more to the man. The last Dominant on the panel is a woman named Ms. Clark, who is stunning with her long, blonde hair, red lips, and sexy business suit.

I'm thrilled when I finish my first lesson. Because Liege filled out my application and claimed I didn't like bald men, I'm partnered with a sexy Dom with no hair to play out the scene. I have no issues with bald men and thoroughly enjoy myself.

The practicum, however, turns out not to be so easy.

"Miss Cox, you say here that you do not like punishment," Headmaster Coen states.

I lower my head. "I do not, Headmaster."

"It should be easy enough to avoid if you simply do as your Dominant commands."

I squirm where I stand, not sure how to answer him.

"Perhaps you could name a tool you find challenging," he suggests.

I immediately blurt, "His belt."

"His belt?"

"I don't like when my Master punishes me with his belt."

"Why do you give him cause to punish you?" Marquis Gray asks.

I look at him and say meekly, "I try not to."

Marquis Gray writes something in his notes, and I feel my heart drop when the trainers start whispering amongst themselves. When they come to an agreement, Headmaster Coen addresses me again.

"We agree that the belt would be an appropriate challenge for you. The Dom we would have normally chosen for such a scene is not here because you failed to fill out the application correctly. However, Master Anderson has offered to scene with you. Is that acceptable?"

Although I want nothing to do with belts, I'm surprised they are asking for my input. Remembering Liege's warning, I instantly consent.

I stand there, alone on the stage, as Master Anderson gets up and leaves the room. He returns fifteen minutes later, no longer dressed in a suit. Instead, he wears only jeans and a cowboy hat. His muscular chest makes my heart flutter but, as soon as he unbuckles his belt and slides it through his belt loops, I feel like crying.

He tells me to strip and ready myself. I obey, holding my breath as I wait for his onslaught.

The trainer surprises me, using the leather belt to caress my skin and stimulate my desire with the gentle touch of the hated tool. I've never dreamed a belt could feel pleasurable. He takes his time, igniting my passion with focused attention on my breasts and pussy as he continues to caress my body. Before he's done, his belt is slick with my wetness. I find myself wanting to know what the stroke of a belt under his control feels like on my ass, and I voice that desire aloud. He grants my wish by manually bringing me to orgasm before giving me several stokes of the belt. The sting of it somehow enhances the last pulses of my climax, and I am left awed by the experience.

Before class ends, Headmaster Coen commands me to join him in his office. I suddenly feel sick, wondering if he is going to kick me out of the program for filling out the form wrong.

The thought of facing Liege tonight if they do has me terrified.

Headmaster Coen opens the door to his office and tells me to take a seat while he moves behind his large desk and sits down. He opens a drawer and pulls out a file with my name on it.

Taking out my application, he places it on the desk before me. "Your honesty is imperative."

I swallow hard and nod.

"Did you fill out this application?"

I know my answer will disqualify me from the Training Center…

I close my eyes with a pained expression, building up the courage to answer him. "No, Headmaster."

"Who did?"

"I wrote down what my Master told me to."

He makes a *tsking* sound, and I open my eyes. I'm surprised to see a look of compassion on his face instead of anger. "This course is meant for you, not your Dominant, Miss Cox. Tonight, it was easy to tell that you weren't challenged in the way we were expecting."

I lower my head and the tears start falling. "I'm sorry, Headmaster."

"There is no need to cry," he tells me, handing me a tissue.

I take it from him and ask hesitantly, "Are you going drop me from the program?"

"I need to ask you a few more questions."

I tremble in fear, but I nod.

He pulls out a note, and I instantly recognize Liege's handwriting. He looks it over with a critical expression. "Are you happy as a submissive?"

I falter when I answer him, wondering if it is meant as a trick question. "I want…to do better."

"Let me rephrase that. Are you happy under your Master's care?"

The tears suddenly threaten to start up again, and I shake my head.

"Then why do you wear his collar?"

I look at him in confusion because the answer seems obvious. "He collared me."

Headmaster Coen sits back in his chair. "Explain the history between you two."

I look at him with concern. "I can't."

"Why not?"

I stare at the floor. Everything in me wants to tell him, but I care about my parents too much.

"Rest assured, everything you tell me will remain between us, unless you say otherwise."

I start shaking, terrified I am making a mistake when I start telling him about Liege. How we met online, the tasks he had me do, and what happened after I came to visit him here, including the fact he's locked up my purse and phone until I'm trained properly.

Headmaster Coen nods throughout my explanation but does not comment until I am done.

"You mentioned you were looking for a distraction when you agreed to be his sub. What exactly were you running from, Miss Cox?"

Ethan's face suddenly comes to mind, and I embarrass myself by sobbing. After wads of tissues, I finally calm myself enough to share about Ethan and his tragic death.

The Headmaster surprises me by standing up and holding out his muscular arms to me. I walk into his embrace, feeling safe in those strong arms.

"You have suffered greatly."

I nod, unable to speak without crying again.

He pulls away and looks at me with sympathy. "Do you wish to continue with your training here?"

I gaze up at him and beg, "Please don't make me leave."

He furrows his brow, saying nothing for several moments before walking back to his desk and sitting down. Opening the drawer, he pulls out a fresh application. He picks up the old one and throws it in the trash, sliding the new one in front of me.

"I need you to fill this out tonight."

"I will," I promise.

"Fine." He picks up the phone.

"Rachael, I need you to book a room for Miss Cox at the Grand and charge it to my account."

I shake my head. "No! I must go home with Liege."

He covers the speaker of the phone and asks, "What will happen if you do not?"

"He'll…" I close my eyes, drowning in shame. "He says he'll send the sex tapes to my parents."

Headmaster Coen's eyes narrowed. "Where are the tapes?"

"In his apartment."

"Fine. We'll take care of that. You should have them in your possession tonight."

I stare at him in disbelief as I listen to his conversation. "Let me know when Mr. Liege arrives to pick her up. Tell the man I want to speak with him personally."

He hangs up the phone and asks, "Would you write down the address of the apartment?"

I take the pen and paper he gives me and quickly write it down.

Headmaster Coen makes another phone call. "Hello, Baron? Are you free tonight…? Excellent. I have a new student who needs her things delivered to the Grand Hotel. Could you go to this address?" He reads off what I have written. "You'll find her purse and cell phone locked in a drawer next to the computer. Also, there are some personal tapes of Miss Cox that are being used as blackmail. If you could bring them, along with her suitcase in the closet, she should have all she needs." He pauses for a moment as he listens. "That's right. I'll be detaining the man until I hear back from you." After another long pause, he says, "Much appreciated, Baron.

Miss Cox will be greatly relieved to get her things back."

After he hangs up, Headmaster Coen commands, "Come here and kneel."

I walk over and kneel before him, wondering what he is about to do. I stop breathing when I feel his hands around my neck as he unbuckles the collar.

He throws the hated thing in the trashcan and declares, "Liege no longer has power over you."

It feels as if the weight of the world has been lifted from my shoulders, and I look up at him, too grateful for words.

"Head upstairs. Rachael has ordered a car. It is waiting to take you to the hotel. We want to ensure every student has a safe and healthy environment in which to learn." He stands up and hands me the application.

This man has just saved my life, and all I can think to say is, "Thank you."

He nods. "Before you settle in for the night, I suggest you call your family."

I can't contain my happiness and wrapped my small arms around his beefy waist. "Thank you, thank you, thank you!"

An hour later, I am lying on a giant bed in a hotel that overlooks downtown LA. My heart is bursting with joy, but I still look nervously at the door when I hear someone knock—terrified Liege has found me.

"Miss Cox, it's Baron," a deep voice states from the

other side of the door.

I rush over to open it.

An extremely handsome black man stands there, holding my things.

"I don't know how to thank you…" I gush. "Please come in."

He enters and puts his hand on his chest. "It pains my heart to know you have been treated so poorly. When an abuser uses BDSM to exploit someone, it tears at the fabric of this community. I am here to assure you that the man has been dealt with and will *not* harass you again."

I have no idea what Baron had done to Liege, and I don't care. I'm just eternally grateful I am free of him.

"It's late, so I won't keep you any longer," he tells me.

I give him a bow, the way I was taught to at the Training Center tonight and feel my heart flutter as I look up at him.

He graces me with a charming smile. "Take care, Miss Cox. Perhaps we'll get a chance to scene together during your training."

"I would like that," I tell him.

I shut the door slowly after he leaves, not quite believing my luck. Just this morning, I was fighting to survive another day.

As I look out the window at the city, I suddenly have the feeling that Ethan is with me.

I start to cry again.

But this time, they are tears of joy.

Chance Meeting

Captain

2012

I start today, like all the days before it, staring at my reflection in the mirror.

Every scar on my body reminds me of that horrific day. I pick up the leather patch and cover the area where my eye used to be. Half of my face was obliterated when the grenade hit, leaving behind unsightly scars and a sunken cheek and eye socket.

I wear the patch to protect others. I may have grown used to the looks of shock and the quick turning of their heads when adults come across me, but I will never grow used to the look of terror I see in the eyes of the children I pass.

My life ended on the battlefield. The pain of losing my entire battery rips at my soul every second of every day.

If only I had died with my men…

I honor their sacrifice by going to work every day to study satellite photographs for the National Reconnaissance Officer. It is an empty existence, but it is all I've come to know since being rescued and honorably discharged.

I have become hard—a shell of the man I used to be.

The severity of my wounds makes me an outcast, but I understand.

I am the stuff nightmares are made of.

I stand in line for my lunch order, anxious to return to the office. A little girl hides behind her mother, terrified of me.

I'm startled by a familiar voice behind me. "Excuse me, are you Captain Walker?"

I turn to see Gallant standing beside a stunning woman who is much taller than he.

Gallant holds out his hand and shakes mine firmly. "It is good to see you again, Captain."

I nod uncomfortably, feeling the heavy gaze of the woman next to him on me.

"How long has it been, Captain Walker?" he asks cordially.

"A lifetime ago," I answer, looking at my watch and wishing my number would be called.

Gallant turns to the woman beside him and introduces us. "Ena, this is Captain Walker. Captain, this is my wife, Ena."

"It is an honor to meet you, Captain Walker," she says, holding her hand out to me.

I'm taken aback by the gesture. Women avoid any physical contact with me. I take hold of her hand and shake it firmly.

"My husband has only the highest regard for you. Thank you for the difference you made in his life."

I shake my head, saying gruffly, "I did nothing."

"On the contrary," Gallant declares. "You gave me the value of your expertise, both on and off the battle-field. I owe my life to you, Captain."

"You know I disagree," I growl, remembering when he'd come to visit me in the hospital soon after I was rescued. He'd foolishly made a similar claim, and I'd set him straight then by telling him, "If you had been part of my battery, you would be dead."

I look at Gallant now, grateful the man was promoted and reassigned before our battalion was sent out to meet our fate.

"Captain, can you spare a few minutes?" he asks. "I would love to sit down and talk."

"I'd rather not," I answer tersely. Seeing him again only reminds me of the past.

"Please, Captain," Ena begs earnestly.

I find myself moved by her open acceptance of me. It's rare to be treated as if I have no scars, and it is solely because of her that I agree.

During our conversation, Gallant asks about my life since. I explain that I work as an intelligence analyst, but I keep it at that. I learn from him that he is not only married, but also the father of two young girls. He then goes on to share that he works as a teacher at a school called the Submissive Training Center.

"You teach about whips and chains?" I snort, assuming he is joking.

"Among other things," he replies.

I look to his wife, who smiles pleasantly, and decide Gallant must be telling me the truth.

My curiosity piqued, I ask, "What do you train your students for?"

"We help submissives discover their strengths and limits through instruction and practicums."

"It sounds…interesting."

He turns to his wife and says proudly, "We don't often share this with others, but Ena is not simply my wife, but my beloved submissive."

I glance at her and notice the necklace she wears is actually a delicate collar with a lock. "I never would have suspected."

Gallant wraps his arm around his wife. "We choose to live it out quietly because of the children, but I must tell you that the open and honest exchange between a submissive and Dominant has made for a very fulfilling relationship."

I nod, genuinely happy for them, although I can't imagine such a thing.

"Captain Walker," he says, looking at me with a serious expression, "I don't know if you are open to the idea or not, but I would like to invite you to a BDSM club we frequent. You would only come as an observer, but I think you will find what you need there."

I scoff harshly, "And what do I need?"

"Companionship."

It feels as if I have been hit in the chest, having given up hope of that long ago.

"You will find acceptance on a level you do not normally find," Ena assures me.

I respectfully decline the offer. However, Gallant is a stubborn man and persists. "Come with me once. See what's possible. If you don't care for it, I will never ask again."

The idea of having a woman desire my touch is a powerful incentive. Although skeptical, I eventually agree to it.

"Excellent. We'll pick you up at seven."

"Tonight?"

"You always did tell your men that putting things off is for the undecided. Are you undecided?"

I'm slightly irritated to have my words used against me, but I stand behind their truth and answer, "Seven it is, then."

I find The Haven to be an interesting experience. The club itself has a large gathering area in the middle with a crowd of people milling about. Along the peripheral walls are numerous alcoves, each with its own theme and equipment.

What I find most surprising is the openness with which these people express their sexuality. It is unlike anything I've seen before. Many of the women are either naked or dressed in clothes meant to entice.

More notably, they all seem confident in their own skin—which I find highly attractive. I can't help but be turned on, having been alone for so long, and my libido only intensifies when some of the women I pass return my gaze with interest rather than disgust.

As I watch the different scenes play out in each of the alcoves, I find that bondage appeals to me. Yet, there seems to be something missing.

I do not find the whipping and impact sessions erotic, although I appreciate the passionate cries coming from the submissives receiving the attention—their obvious enjoyment is quite stimulating.

However, it isn't until I see a couple playing out what Gallant informs me is pony play that I begin to get interested. The submissive is dressed in an elaborate costume, with a long tail flowing down her shapely ass and a black leather corset that accentuates her curves. She wears a bit in her mouth, with a harness and blinders. When the Dom places a large plume of feathers on her head as decoration, she instantly transforms into a beautiful show horse.

Her Dom connects a lead to the harness and starts her moving around him in a circle, directing her gait with clicks of his tongue. He treats her like a treasured pet, and I find the dynamic between them exciting.

Gallant notices my interest and informs me, "There are many different types of pet play, from puppy and kitten, to fox, bunny, and even cow."

I'm slightly unnerved to discover that this is where my interests lie, but I am encouraged by the fact that others share this kink.

"It makes perfect sense to me," Gallant says, picking up on my discomfort. "You were always supportive and nurturing toward the men under your charge. Those traits don't disappear simply because you're no longer part of the Army."

I watch the submissive proudly prancing in front of her owner, intent on pleasing him as he lightly smacks her with a riding crop to pick up her gait. The way she delights in him rewarding her with praise stirs something profound in me.

I leave The Haven having been deeply affected by the night's events. For the first time since that day on the battlefield, I feel a spark of life.

In the weeks that follow, I visit Gallant after hours and he teaches me how to be a Dominant. Never in a million years would I have ever dreamed this would be the direction my life would take, but I am grateful for his expertise and natural teaching ability.

There comes a point when he claims I'm ready to scene on my own and mentions that he has a student in mind for my first solo experience. "Her name is Brianna Bennett. She's the top student in my class and I'm certain you two would be a good match for each other. Miss Bennet will benefit from an introduction to pet play in preparation for the curriculum we have set for next week."

I'm concerned and ask, "This is not a kink of hers?"

"She cannot say until she experiences it. You must understand, as staff at the Submissive Training Center, we seek to challenge our students so they will have a wealth of experiences to draw from."

"What about my physical condition?" I ask, needing to be blunt. "I am unwilling to couple with a woman who finds me repulsive."

Gallant smiles. "Miss Bennett responds to a man's Dominant nature far more than his looks. That became apparent to the trainers the first day of class. As I said before, I believe this would be a good opportunity for you both."

However, I am not convinced and tell him, "It is one thing to contemplate scening on my own, but quite another to actually go through with it."

Gallant clasps me on the shoulder. "Agreed. And that time has come, Captain."

I go to the Submissive Training Center, prepared to bid for a woman who is voluntarily gifting her submission to another while gaining nothing other than the experience.

I glance over at Gallant, who has come to witness the auction. He nods his head confidently; still certain we make a good match.

I have taken a few precautions for our first meeting, needing to assure myself that this is what Miss Bennett truly wants. I cannot endure a look of revulsion nor do I want her to suffer if my appearance proves too much for her.

To start, I have her blindfolded before the auction begins.

After a spirited bidding war, I go to collect her from the stage. Without saying a word, I lead her down the hallway to the room Gallant has reserved. As we walk together, I take the opportunity to look her over. She's comely, with nice curves and long brown hair. Although I prefer blondes, I find her exceptionally attractive.

I take her to the room and leave her there, shutting the door behind me. Inside I have left instructions for her to follow, as well as an outfit I have chosen for the evening.

Heading to the bar at the hotel where I've reserved a room, I sit and wait in the corner. Twenty minutes later, Miss Bennett enters the barroom wearing the little black dress and the red rose tucked into her hair, just as I have instructed.

She looks exquisite in that dress and men at the bar take notice as she takes a seat. The bartender has been instructed to give her my gift, and he hands her the small box.

I watch with interest as Miss Bennett opens it and takes out the delicate silver chain. She reads the note inside, which states she is to wear the bracelet signifying her acceptance of the chain that binds her to me for the evening.

I watch with satisfaction as she puts it on her wrist. She looks around, wondering if I am there.

I continue to wait.

Soon, an attractive man approaches and begins talking to her. I move closer, wanting to hear what's being said between them.

"The flower is a nice touch," the man states.

Brie touches the rose in her hair and replies, "It is beautiful. Thank you."

I know by her answer that she thinks he is her Dom, and I wonder how this will play out.

"What should I call you?" she asks him.

The man grins, telling her his name and asking her if she wants to leave.

She agrees shyly, still unaware she is talking to the wrong man.

It's obvious the guy can't believe his luck and is anxious to fuck her when he says, "Don't bother finishing that drink."

I move in when I see her start to stand and place my hand on her shoulder, commanding her to remain seated.

I feel her tremble under my hand.

The man puffs out his chest. "Look, buddy. You get your hands off the girl. She's coming with me."

"No, she is not. Ask her."

Worried that he is about to lose her to me, the man tells Brie, "Give me the word and I'll be happy to deck this guy."

I am encouraged when she replies, "I'm sorry...this man is my blind date."

"This freak is your date?" he growls angrily.

I expect Miss Bennett to turn around, wanting to see what I look like based on his response, but she tells him firmly, "It would be best if you leave now."

"I concur," I tell him with a smirk. "Your presence is not welcomed. Please leave."

The man cannot believe he's about to lose this beautiful woman to the likes of me and cries out in disbelief,

"You *can't* be serious! You'd rather go out with this sideshow act than me?"

Brie bows her head, ignoring him.

I take her hand and guide her out of the bar, feeling great satisfaction as I listen to the man cursing behind me.

Miss Bennett instantly apologizes, her eyes still cast down.

"I found it amusing, or I wouldn't have let it continue," I tell her. I turn Brie, so she is facing me, and command, "Look at me."

I wait to see a hint of revulsion on her face and am ready to end the evening, sparing us both a miserable night.

Her gaze slowly travels from my torso up to my face, and I watch as she studies the severe scars on my face with curiosity.

Before she can ask, I tell her, "Injury. You will not speak of it."

She accepts my answer and asks, "What shall I call you?"

"What my men did. Captain."

"Yes, Captain," she replies, smiling warmly.

Gallant was correct. She appears to be a good fit, so I guide her to the elevator and tell her as we wait, "The cretin was correct. The flower is a nice touch. You look lovely, pet."

Her smile widens, and she thanks me for the clothes and bracelet.

Wanting to be clear on how the night will play out, I explain, "I like my pets to wear a reminder of their position."

"It is beautifully effective, Captain."

Her answer pleases me.

I walk her into the hotel room and immediately take charge, unzipping her dress and watching it slip from her body and down to the floor. It leaves her wearing only stockings, shoes and a bra. I'm impatient to see her naked chest and remove the bra next. Her breasts are full and inviting and, as her Master, I have the liberty of playing with them until she is wet with need.

I kiss her shoulder lightly before kneeling to attach a metal cuff to her ankle. "You will remain chained to the bed for the duration of our time together."

I take off my shirt and am aware of her stare as she takes in the many shrapnel scars that cover my chest. I am unprepared when she asks, "May I kiss them, Captain?"

Not emotionally equipped for such a request, I respond defensively, telling her I would have preferred the blonde at the auction. It is unkind, but the reaction comes out of shock. I refuse to be vulnerable with this girl.

She doesn't get upset. Instead, she replies in a solemn tone, "I have found that the outer shell doesn't matter much."

I choke up, surprised to have this young woman remind me what I already know to be true—and I feel ashamed. "Touché."

I pat my knee and tell her to kneel at my feet.

I spend the evening petting her hair and handfeeding her from my plate, enjoying the freedom to pamper the young woman in this way. Eventually, however, my need to possess her body wins out.

Being a long time since slipping my cock into a woman, I do not hold back, pounding her long and hard until she orgasms.

She enjoys the roughness of my unbridled passion, crying out, "O Captain, my Captain!" as I come. I give her a well-deserved slap on the ass for being so cheeky after I climax, then lie on top of her and feel the welcomed caress of her pussy as she comes around my cock after being thoroughly fucked.

Afterward, I roll off and lie beside her.

I have not felt like a man in a long time and I am grateful to this beautiful submissive. Her honest joy in bringing me pleasure has opened me up enough to be vulnerable to her.

"You may lick them," I tell her quietly.

She smiles as she gets on all fours and tenderly ministers to each scar. The gesture is overwhelming, and I say nothing, but I covet the healing power of her gentle caresses.

When she leaves to go back to the Training Center for debriefing with her peers, I get out the evaluation form and fill it out while my feelings are still fresh.

Trusted her instincts in lieu of her Master's wishes. In my case, it was exactly what I needed. Truly a beauty in mind and spirit.

After my encounter with Miss Bennett, I begin exploring my dominant needs more seriously at The Haven. I find that the power exchange between a Dominant and a submissive is highly addictive.

Since the dynamic does not require an emotional connection, I do not have to concern myself with the unwanted strings that come with commitment. It is a mutually safe environment for both parties involved. As my reputation grows, I find more and more subs asking to scene with me, despite my looks and age.

When Gallant calls a few months later with another auction, I tell him with all honesty that I'm not interested. "I'm doing well enough on my own."

"But, Captain, this wouldn't be for your benefit. The girl needs you."

"Why would you say that?"

"Her fantasy is one she's never experienced herself, but it is the reason she sought out BDSM to begin with."

"And that is?"

"I cannot share with you unless you intend to bid for her."

"Surely, you could ask other Doms with far more experience than me."

"I could, but she's a special case. She needs someone with your nurturing and supportive nature."

"I think you're giving me more credit than I deserve."

"Once you read her fantasy, I know you will agree," he insists.

When I remain unconvinced, he asks me, "Is it the auction price?"

"No," I laugh. "I have plenty in the bank. Remember, I don't have a family to support, and I'm a man with simple needs."

Even though I doubt I am the right man, Gallant is not someone to ask frivolously, so I agree to attend the auction and make a bid for his sake. However, I do not plan to win.

Once I receive the girl's fantasy from the Training Center, I understand why Gallant has been so adamant. The scene she's written in her fantasy journal is one I am destined to play out. As I read about her desires on the page, I already have in mind how I will set up the initial meeting…

On the day of the auction, I stand in the back and look over the other Doms in attendance while a slip of a girl wearing a blindfold is escorted onto the stage.

She looks so fragile up there that I begin to have doubts.

"Miss Cox is twenty, currently working as a waitress in LA, but plans to continue her bachelor's degree in marketing. Her trainers describe her as shy but pliable."

I see her lick her lips nervously, and a profound need to protect this woman overtakes me as I watch the other Doms stare at her with lust. I do not know their intentions, but I am certain of mine, so I start with a high bid.

The bidding quickly escalates as a muscle-bound Dom decides he must have her. I will not allow it and raise my bid to nine hundred, looking over at him with a confident smile.

He increases his bid by another hundred, but I immediately follow suit and he shakes his head, unable to match it.

"Going once…going twice…sold to the man in the back."

The losing Dom glares at me as I make my way to the stage. As I pass by, he says under his breath, "She deserves better than you."

I look at him and say nothing. While he may be right, I'm certain I am a hell of a better match for her than he is.

I walk up the stairs to the stage, looking at her more closely as I approach. She has an elfin quality about her—petite, with gossamer hair, pink lips, and an air of innocence I find charming. I lead her off the stage with my hand resting on her back, guiding her to the private room.

Just as I had with Miss Bennett, I leave her there and shut the door. There, she will find a card with a set of instructions, along with the outfit I have picked out for her to wear.

I prefer starting these auction encounters this way, since I am unfamiliar with the submissives. It allows me to observe them while they don't know I'm watching.

I leave the Center, holding her gift in my hand. Now, it's up to Miss Cox to decide how the rest of this evening will go…

First Auction

Candy

I feel nervous when I hear the door shut behind me. Wondering if the Dom who won the auction will return, I wait for several minutes before finally untying my blindfold.

I squeal with joy when I see a beautiful floral dress and pretty pink shoes laid out for me. Whoever this mystery Dom is, he has a romantic heart.

I notice an envelope with my name on it, and I pick it up to read the contents.

> Get dressed for me and take the cab that is waiting for you outside.
>
> You are to enter the pet store and wait for me by the kittens for sale.

I can barely contain my excitement, charmed by the idea of meeting him at a pet shop to begin our time together. After I get dressed in the adorable outfit, the cabbie takes me to a pet shop across town.

I walk into the shop and head directly to the penned area where the kittens are playing on a multi-layered cat structure. I love watching them, and I giggle when one of the kittens takes a flying leap but misses, tumbling to the ground.

From behind me, I hear a low chuckle. "He has an ambitious spirit."

I know it must be my mystery Dom and turn around slowly. The older gentleman wears an eyepatch and half his face is scarred, but my breath actually catches when our eyes meet. The intensity of his gaze captivates me, and I am reminded of Ethan.

"Miss Cox?"

I smile. "Mystery Dom?"

He nods. The intense green of his good eye is a color I have never seen before, and I can't stop staring.

"What are you thinking?" he asks in a gruff voice.

"Your eyes…" I blush hard and immediately correct myself. "I mean, your eye is such an unusual color of green. It's mesmerizing. I apologize for staring." I lower my head, mortified at myself.

He puts his finger under my chin, lifting my head to meet his gaze again. "Relax. I am not easily offended."

I blush a deeper shade of red and nod gratefully.

"This gift is for you." He gives me the thin box he holds in his hand.

I lift the lid and let out a delighted squeak when I see a silver headband with the delicate cat ears outlined with sparkly crystals. He takes it from the box and carefully places it on my head.

"Perfect," he states, looking at me with satisfaction.

I'm gratified by his praise and smile up at him as I touch the pretty headband with my fingertips. I never expected a gift.

"Thank you, …?" I pause, unsure of his name.

"Captain. You will call me what my men called me, Miss Cox."

"Thank you, Captain." The title suits him and explains the terrible scars he carries. It makes me adore the man even more.

"I was thinking a cat toy would be a good purchase before we leave."

I can't believe I have partnered with someone so romantically sweet and willing to play out my unusual fantasy. He guides me to the cat section and tells me to pick whichever item catches my interest.

I look over the huge selection of toys, feeling like a kid in a candy shop, and finally decide on a pole with pink feathers on the end of the string.

"Excellent choice," he compliments, taking it up to the cash register. The cashier looks at him strangely while ringing up the purchase but says nothing as Captain escorts me out of the pet shop.

He leads me to a big, military-green vehicle, and I have to smile to myself. It looks like an Army truck to me. Captain gives me his hand for support as I get into the large vehicle—and, again, I am reminded of Ethan.

During the drive, he explains, "I don't normally take submissives to my home, but it didn't seem right to take my pet to a hotel."

Pet…

My heart flutters when he calls me that. I can't contain the joy I feel, and tears suddenly well up in my eyes. I try to blink them away, but Captain notices.

"Is everything okay, Miss Cox?"

I smile, nodding my head. "I'm so happy right now."

He returns the smile, then looks back at the road.

"Captain?"

Keeping his eyes forward, he asks, "Yes?"

"My heart is beating so fast right now because this is my first time."

He frowns, looking concerned. "For what?"

"To be someone's pet. This is something I've dreamed about ever since…" I stop as visions of Liege's face come to mind.

Unaware of my past, Captain asks, "How, exactly, did you find that you liked this particular fetish?"

Keeping my answer simple, I tell him, "I read about it on a website. Well, not exactly. I read a post by a Dom who was talking about his pet. It was so sweet, and it stirred something inside me. I just knew, right then and there. Ever since, I have dreamed about a scene like this, so thank you for being willing to play out my fantasy."

"There is no need to thank me. You and I share similar interests."

I cock my head, looking at him questioningly.

He keeps his attention on the road, stating, "Your fetish is my fetish."

I bite my lip, thrilled beyond words.

I'm anxious to learn more about him and ask respectfully, "May I ask how you came to know pet play was your kink, Captain?"

"A good friend took me to a club and I naturally gravitated toward it. Never knew there was such a thing until that night."

I grin, grateful to be partnered with someone so compatible.

He pulls up to a small house and helps me out of the car. I'm all nerves as he unlocks the door to his home and ushers me inside.

Captain's home is comfortable but sparsely decorated and tidy, exactly what I would expect from a military man.

"This is very nice…" I tell him as he leads me to the couch in the main room.

"I'm not one for the frills, but I know what I like."

"I like a man who knows what he likes," I answer, then blush, knowing how cheesy I sound.

He sits down beside me and cradles my cheek. "Tonight, you are my pet, my beloved companion."

My heart melts.

"From this moment forward, you will act naturally as the treasured kitten you are. My only expectation is that you willingly obey your master. If, for any reason, you wish to stop, call out your safeword."

Instantly, Captain has made me feel cherished and safe.

"Do you understand?"

Having carefully listened to his instructions, I nod and let out a little mew.

He smiles. "Excellent."

Captain stands up and asks me to join him. I tremble as his hands caress my skin and he slowly undresses me.

With my clothes on the floor, he lightly runs his hands over my hard nipples and down to my buttocks. His gentle touch turns me on and I purr softly.

"You are missing something," he informs me.

I watch as he picks up a pink collar with a jingly bell from the side table and places it around my neck. "This is a temporary collar, only meant for tonight."

I get pleasurable goosebumps when he secures it around my neck. Afterward, he steps back to look at me, dressed only in my pet collar and cat ears.

"You are exquisite, my pet."

I look at him adoringly and purr.

"I bet you're thirsty after such a long day. Let me get you some milk."

I watch Captain walk to the kitchen and return moments later with a golden pet bowl. He places it on the floor and sits back down on the couch.

"Now, drink, my pet. But keep your eyes on me while you do."

I get down on all fours and lean down to lap the milk like a dainty kitten as I look at Captain. His hungry gaze travels over my body, but mine never leaves his face.

Studying the undamaged side of Captain's face, I can tell he was an extremely handsome man. Truly, he still is.

His gaze meets mine again as I sensually lick the milk. There is an intoxicating chemistry between us, and I find myself already aching for him.

When Captain unbuckles his belt, the sound makes my heart beat faster. I watch with excitement as he unbuttons his pants and slowly unzips them. I stop lapping momentarily as he pulls out his rigid shaft and starts stroking it. Captain is a generously endowed man.

"Pet…"

I suddenly realize my mistake. Purring my approval of his manly asset, I continue lapping my milk, totally aroused as I watch him stroke that hard cock which will be stroking me inside before the night is out.

When I finish with my milk, I crawl over to him and playfully rub my cheek against his leg.

He pulls me up between his legs. "Lick your Master," he orders.

I take a tentative lick of his smooth head and take pleasure when I hear his husky groan. I take little licks up and down his shaft before I take him into my mouth. When he cups the back of my head and begins directing my movements, I feel a gush of wetness between my legs.

I love being under his control as he teaches me without words how he likes his cock sucked. With one hand directing me, he uses the other to play with my hair, sending delightful tingles down my spine as I please him.

But Captain doesn't come.

Instead, he pulls my mouth from his cock and picks me up, carrying me to his bedroom. Laying me gently on the bed, he begins to undress.

I watch as he kicks off his shoes before slowly unbuttoning his shirt to reveal a toned chest covered in scars and salt-and-peppery chest hair. He then takes off his pants, briefs and socks, laying them on the side table before facing me in all his naked glory.

Captain is a sexy silver fox, and his hot body—scars and all—stirs my inner animal.

I get on all fours and wiggle my ass, moaning seductively like a cat in heat as I stare at him.

He shakes his head. "Oh, pet, you have your Master horny as hell."

Captain pulls me to the edge of the bed and slides a condom on before he rubs his shaft against my wet pussy. I lower my chest and look back at him, beseeching him with my eyes to take me.

He groans as his pushes his cock into me, filling my tight pussy. I meow seductively, rotating my hips as he sinks deeper into me.

"Damn…" he growls as he grabs my hips and pushes all the way in, holding me there.

My body is on fire, waiting for the pounding to begin, but he pulls out.

I look at him and pout, wiggling my ass again, *needing* to be penetrated.

Captain shakes his head, warning me, "I want to pound you so hard right now, you may have to use your safeword."

I purr, clutching the bed cover in anticipation.

Captain grabs my hips again, and I close my eyes as he enters me with one solid stroke. I bite my lip as he begins thrusting, each stroke long and deep. His cock demands I relax enough to take him, and I want it—I want to be claimed by him!

I howl in lustful pleasure as he begins to ramp up, pounding me so deep I am aware of nothing else but the strokes of his cock. The bell on my collar rings merrily with each thrust while the slapping sound of skin against skin fills the room.

Captain suddenly stops and holds me still. Without warning, my body hits the edge and starts pulsing as I climax. Before I am done, Captain starts up again.

I yowl in ecstasy as he claims me again.

This time, he keeps going past his own edge, stiffening before he comes long and hard deep inside me. Again, another orgasm sneaks up on me, and I come just as his ends.

He collapses beside me, spent.

I just stare at him in wonder.

When he glances over at me and catches me staring, he chuckles. "You never called your safeword."

I shake my head, my bell tinkling prettily.

"Come here, you sexy kitten." Captain pulls me close and holds me in his arms. I lie there in complete contentment, my soul flying high.

Captain begins stroking my hair. "When I read your fantasy, I was entranced. Now that I have you in my arms, I am doubly so."

I purr against his chest, feeling equally captivated by this man.

Eventually, he gets up to clean off and comes back, a towel wrapped around his waist.

"Clean up, my pet, and lie on the cat pillow beside the couch while I whip up something to eat."

After freshening up, I lie down on the soft pillow while I listen to Captain cooking and smell delicious aromas wafting from his kitchen.

He walks out a short time later, carrying a plate and fork. He lays it on the coffee table, then orders me to come and sit on the floor beside him.

I lean against his leg and stare at the plate.

"I thought, what better nourishment for my sexy kitten than some fresh fish?"

Captain breaks off a tender, flaky layer of the salmon with his fork and feeds it to me. The taste of lemon melds well with the subtle sweetness of the fish. I purr in pleasure after swallowing it.

I watch as he takes his own bite and winks at me. With a romantic flare, he hand-feeds me, sharing the entire plate with me. Afterward, he picks up the feather toy I picked out and swings it in the air.

I'm in a frisky mood and playfully bat at the feathers, caught up in the simple joy of it. Captain's low chuckle as I pounce and capture it warms me inside.

Our partnership is easy and natural, both of us fulfilled in the roles we have chosen.

After my frolic, I can see that Captain's expression has changed. The look in his eye is one of desire. I crawl over to him and lay my head in his lap, looking up at him with need.

He pets my head and asks in a low, husky voice, "Are you ready for me to challenge you again?"

In answer, I move up and give him a light kiss on the nose.

He grabs the back of my head, kissing me deeply as his tongue explores my mouth.

Captain's passion seems unquenchable as he carries me back to his bedroom and we spend the next few hours pleasing each other.

Defending Her

Captain

It's been weeks since I've seen Candy and am surprised when I spot her at The Haven, along with the trainers of the Submissive Training Center. It appears her class is being introduced to the club by the staff of the school, and she has been slated to scene with Tono Ren Nosaka, the Kinbaku artist.

I hang back to watch her scene with the bondage master.

A large crowd has gathered, and I catch a glimpse of Miss Bennett among the multitude. We all watch with anticipation as Nosaka finishes adjusting his knots before lifting Candy into the air.

It is truly an inspiring sight, seeing the look of ecstasy on her face as she slowly twirls in the air, suspended in the beauty of his jute. The Japanese Master has created something truly beautiful with his intricate knots, making her look like a stunning piece of art.

Nosaka whispers to Candy as his hands glide over

her body, adjusting the knots. She's in an almost trace-like state, wearing a relaxed smile on her lips as she twists in the air above the jute mat. She seems the perfect canvas for his artistry, and I am both turned on and inspired watching them scene together.

I leave before she notices me but, eventually, Candy finds me later that evening. "Captain, I just had to come and say hi. I can't tell you how happy I am to see you here!" She bows her head, unable to hide the smile on her lips.

I am humbled that she has sought me out. "It is a pleasure to see you again, Miss Cox."

"I wanted to thank you again for the most incredible evening of my life, and for the wonderful evaluation. All my classmates were jealous."

"My evaluation was fair and honest."

She blushes. "I was deeply honored by your praise, Captain."

I find everything about this girl alluring. It's a damn shame my age and condition preclude me from pursuing her.

However, I am grateful for our auction encounter, a rare opportunity the Submissive Training Center's unique curriculum has afforded me. "I'm glad to hear you enjoyed our time together, Miss Cox."

Her eyes flash with excitement. "I did, Captain. To be honest, I can't stop thinking about it."

Oh, that I was twenty years younger, I think to myself.

Rather than commenting on her last statement, I tell her, "I trust you are doing well with your studies?"

She grins. "I love the Training Center! It's the best

thing that has ever happened to me."

"Good." I look at my watch, wanting to let her interact with the other Dominants. "Well, I'd better let you go. It's time you start introducing yourself to the other Doms in attendance."

She smiles shyly. "Actually, Captain, I'd prefer to spend time with you, if that's okay?"

I give her a rare smile, touched by her misguided compassion. She should not concern herself with me when she has the chance to mingle with better-suited Dominants. "Miss Cox, you have a golden opportunity here. Don't waste it on an old man."

She wraps her arm around mine. "Please, Captain."

I shake my head, wearing an amused smile as I lead her to the bar in the center of the club. Since she does not wear a collar, sitting here will give other Dominants the opportunity to approach her while we talk.

As I guide her to a seat, I inadvertently brush the fresh scar on the back of her shoulder. I'd noticed it the night we scened together, but I had thought nothing of it.

I order two lime and sodas, wanting to avoid alcohol so we both remain clearheaded. "I saw you with the Kinbaku master earlier," I mention casually.

"You did?"

"I was not the only one. It was a well-attended scene. I must say, you looked breathtaking suspended in rope."

"Tonight was an amazing experience," she says with a light blush. "Tono Nosaka is a talented artist, and he's so humble and gentle."

"He is, and I noticed you two worked well together."

I want to point Candy in the direction of Masters I hold in high regard.

A Dominant comes up to introduce himself to Candy. While they talk, I glance at her bare shoulder, taking a closer look at the scar.

A cold chill runs through my veins.

I've seen that type of scar before. I know exactly what causes it because Grapes was covered in those scars.

After the Dom leaves, I ask her, "Who gave you that scar, Miss Cox?"

Candy looks at me self-consciously, shaking her head. "It doesn't matter, Captain."

"Who did this?" I repeat, unwillingly to let it go.

"No one you know…" she answers, evading my direct question.

"Tell me, pet," I reply in a gentler tone, genuinely concerned for her.

Candy looks at me with shame in her eyes and whispers, "It was someone I was collared to."

Instantly, my blood pressure shoots up. "Why would he do such a thing?"

"He wanted to improve my endurance."

"This is clearly abuse." I growl angrily.

Seeing my concern, Candy caresses my scarred cheek. "Captain. Headmaster Coen handled the situation. I'm okay now. It's okay."

"It's *not* okay," I insist.

"It was my fault." She looks down, unwilling to look me in the eye. "I was stupid and let a guy I didn't really know collar me."

"This is not your fault." I can't stand the idea of anyone hurting her, much less someone claiming authority over her as a Dom. "The wrong lies entirely with him."

Tears fill her eyes. "But I shouldn't have been so foolish. I was stupid to trust him."

I put my finger to her lips. "Enough with calling yourself stupid. It stops now."

When she nods, I remove my finger. "There is no excuse for what that man did. It is morally wrong to abuse anyone, much less a submissive you have collared and promised to care for. The man needs to be severely corrected."

"It's been taken care of. Baron said so himself."

I'm resolute about confronting the man who did this to her, and she can read it on my face.

"There's no need to get involved. Liege is a part of my past I don't want to ever think about him again."

Liege is his name…

I'm already planning to contact Baron tomorrow and will find out everything he knows. I need to meet up with this man and personally express how I feel about what he has done.

But I can see Candy is distressed, so I let it go for the moment. Holding up my glass, I toast her. "To your future, Miss Cox. May you be free of wannabe Doms from this day forward."

She clinks my glass, relief showing on her face.

I may appear calm, but inside I am boiling with rage as I stare at that scar on her shoulder.

Liege betrayed the trust of an innocent. There is no greater wrong, and I will be the man to teach him the error of his ways.

Several days later, I finally have the chance to meet up with Baron and get the information I need.

But he warns me, "The man is a tool. I wouldn't want you doing something that might get you in jail. He isn't worth it."

"Don't worry, Baron. As a former Captain in the Army, I would never let my actions dishonor my country."

"I assumed as much but needed to give you that friendly warning. While I am certain I got the message across, I have no issues with you checking in on him."

"I want to thank you for helping Miss Cox. It's upsetting to think of someone young and innocent being treated in such an unconscionable manner. It makes my blood boil."

Baron agrees, telling me, "I feel the same, which is why I've made it my mission to go to clubs on the weekends looking for men like him. Assholes who are trying to take advantage of inexperienced submissives. I feel it is my duty to rid the BDSM community of any abusive impostors I see."

"It is a worthy endeavor, Baron." I feel nothing but respect for this Dom. As I get up to leave, I give him a firm handshake. "It's an honor to know there are people like you protecting this community."

"I feel a debt of gratitude, myself. You've sacrificed

so much protecting our country. Thank you, Captain." The look of admiration in Baron's eyes makes me highly uncomfortable.

I nod curtly. "I wish I could have done more."

With the address in my hand, I drive directly to Liege's apartment, having been informed that the man never leaves it. My mind is already conjuring visions of what that man did to Candy, and I have to control the fury raging inside me.

I walk up seven flights of stairs after finding out the elevator is broken. Each step only increases my rage as I pass old trash, broken bottles and discarded needles on the staircase.

The thought that Candy was forced to live in these conditions infuriates me.

When I finally reach the apartment, I take a moment to put on gloves before I pound on the door. When I get no answer, I pound even harder. Eventually, I hear the lock being slid back, then the door partially opens. As soon as I see the scrawny, long-haired bastard, I push hard against the door and let myself in.

"What the hell?" he cries. "Get the fuck out of my apartment, dude."

I survey the small apartment and am horrified to see a young woman cowering in the corner next to a metal-framed bed.

"Miss, gather your things. You're coming with me."

She glances at the boy in fear.

"She's not going anywhere with you!" Liege shouts.

I ignore him and tell her, "I will ensure your safety." In a reassuring tone, I repeat, "Now, go get your things."

I turn my attention back on Liege. "I'm here on behalf of Miss Cox. You remember her, don't you? An innocent girl who made the mistake of trusting you."

"I have no idea what you are talking about."

I wrap my hand around his throat and push him against the wall. "The hell you don't. She wasn't looking to get involved with BDSM, but you found her online and manipulated her into thinking you were a Dom. Am I right?"

"Let...go of...me," he chokes out, his eyes bulging with fear.

"You lied to her, telling her things you knew nothing about in the hopes she would believe you—and she did. Do you know why?" I get right up in his face. "She was an innocent, and you betrayed that innocence." I start squeezing his throat, watching him struggle helplessly. I may be an old man, but he's no match for me.

His face turns bright red as he starts making gurgling sounds. I release my hold just enough to let the air flow back in, but I keep my grip tight on the bastard's throat.

"You are nothing but a sniveling coward, physically abusing women claiming it's BDSM. By lying about who you are, you've pissed off the wrong people. We don't look kindly on abuse." I look toward the girl, who now holds a small bag in her hands. "Even worse, this is the second girl you've held against her will."

"She came of her own free will!" Liege looks at the

girl and demands, "Isn't that right?"

She nods her head fearfully.

"Are you delusional? This girl did not give you consent. I suspect you purposely misrepresented who you were, then threatened her into staying here—just like Miss Cox. You are the lowest of the low."

His eyes widen as I squeeze his throat harder. I suddenly let go and push Liege to the floor, turning him onto his stomach. I pull a rope out of my pocket and have him hogtied before he even knows what's happening.

He lies there gasping for breath, stunned.

I turn to the young lady again. "Miss, a Dominant's level of care reflects his level of experience. As you can see…" I look down at Liege struggling on the floor. "…this sniveling bastard is not a Dominant in any sense of the word. You have been lied to and owe no allegiance to him."

I glare at the boy grunting like a pig as he squirms in his bonds. "And he won't be deceiving anyone else."

I go to his computer and insert my flash drive. I set the program to work collecting data. By the time I'm done analyzing the information I've gathered here today, I will know everything about the man. It will give me the means to ensure he never attempts this with anyone else.

While I wait, Liege curses me, but the hogtie ensures he can't take in enough air to expend any energy, so he's soon back to grunting like a pig—an appropriate sound for the bastard.

After I have all the data, I take out the flash drive and look down at him. "I'll be watching your every move no matter where you are. One misstep, and I won't hesitate to exact my own brand of justice—it won't be pretty." I toss a dull table knife on the floor just out of his reach. With some diligence, he should be able to cut himself free before the night is through.

I glance at the girl and notice she is staring at Liege in fear, even in this helpless state. It concerns me, so I walk over to remove the cheap dog collar from her neck and throw it to the floor in disgust.

"You're free. He can't hurt you again."

The girl stares at me with the look of a frightened rabbit. I know my appearance is terrifying, so I explain, "Old war wounds. I'm going to make sure you make it back home." I hold out my hand to take her bag from her.

"Don't do it, cumwhore," Liege warns from the floor.

I give him a swift kick to the side, not breaking eye contact with the girl. She holds out her small bag to me with a trembling hand.

"There's nothing to be scare of," I assure her. "I may be ugly, but I would fight to the death to make sure you make it home safely."

She nods and takes my other hand like a little child. I grasp it firmly, grateful for her trust. I guide her out of the apartment to the sound of Liege gasping out profanities.

As I'm shutting the door, I look back and tell him in a voice loaded with malice, "*Never* again."

Heading down the long flight of stairs, I ask her, "What's your name?"

She automatically mumbles under her breath, "Cumwhore."

I stop and turn to face her, growling, "No, that is not your name."

Tears fill her eyes as she backs away, wrapping her hands around herself. She is scared. It is critical I not let the rage I feel toward Liege show in my tone or expression.

I start again, asking in a gentler tone, "What is your real name?"

She replies quietly, as if afraid to speak it. "Anna Lynne."

Holding out my hand to shake hers, I give her a warm smile. "It is a pleasure to meet you, Miss Lynne. People call me Captain."

She hesitantly shakes my hand, still clearly frightened of me.

"I have a feeling you have family worried about you."

She nods as tears start streaming down her cheeks.

"Where do you live?"

"Kansas," she chokes out.

I'm shocked to hear she is so far from home, having assumed she was living in the area. "Why don't you call them while I drive you to the airport?"

For the first time, I see hope in her eyes. "You're buying me a ticket home?"

"Yes. You'll be seeing your family soon."

She looks at me in disbelief, then takes my hand again, ready to leave this nightmare behind. Once we are out of the apartment building, I walk her over to my vehicle and hand her my cell phone.

However, she seems reluctant to take it from me. "My parents are going to be mad at me."

"You know how relieved they'll be, hearing your voice? It will override any other emotion."

She stares at the phone sadly. "But I don't want them to know what happened."

"Miss Lynne, you can tell them whatever you're comfortable with. This first phone call is simply to let them know you are safe and will be coming home today."

She looks at me in surprise. "It took two weeks hitchhiking for me to get here."

I shudder to think what could have happened to such a young girl on her way here and feel the overwhelming need to get her back home as quickly as possible. "I'll get you on the first flight back," I promise.

She glances up at the apartment building.

I see the lingering fear in Anna's eyes and reassure her, "That boy won't ever contact you again. I'll be closely monitoring him, and I vow to do whatever it takes to keep him from hurting you or anyone else."

She looks up at my scarred face and, in a trembling voice, she says, "I trust you."

"Good, then let me help you into the car so you can make that call while I drive us to the airport."

She sits in the seat, a fresh bruise visible on her throat.

I'm seething inside, knowing that Candy, as well as this girl, was abused by this man under the guise of BDSM. I start the car and head out, listening to her emotional phone call to her parents.

It's enough to tear at a man's soul. Knowing that Candy and her parents suffered the same thing only hurts me that much more.

After Anna hangs up, she seems despondent.

"Miss Lynne, I know you said you're reluctant to speak with your parents about what happened, but I trust in time you will. But, if you find you can't, I strongly advise you to speak to a professional. Someone you can be completely open with. Keeping this inside will only hurt you, and we don't want that."

Anna begins sobbing uncontrollably as all the bottled-up emotions caused by what she's endured erupt at once. I can't stomach the painful cries of another innocent. It eats me up inside. The only comfort I have is knowing that she is safe and headed home.

Two hours later, with her plane ticket in hand, I watch as Anna goes through security and disappears into the crowd.

A life restored.

I walk back to my car, taking solace in knowing Anna will be reunited with her family, but I still feel sick, aware that there are countless other women giving their trust and submission to abusers like this man.

I call Baron and relate what I've done.

"I can't believe Liege took another submissive," Baron says, his voice strained with guilt.

"Don't blame yourself. There are some men who don't learn, but I can guarantee it won't happen again."

I head home, having no intentions of telling Candy about my actions today. This came purely from my driving need to protect.

Now, Candy can move on with her life, truly free from that bastard's influence.

Collar Me

Candy

I can't believe it.

Six weeks at the Submissive Training Center have flown by and, today, I'm facing graduation, but I'm not ready to leave this place—I'm having too much fun here!

When I think of the scared, confused girl I was when I came here, compared to who I am now, I'm in shock at the difference. Under the thoughtful care and guidance of my trainers, I've become confident in who I am and what I want in life.

Gone is the girl seeking escape. I am ready to live my life to the fullest and I know, without a doubt, Ethan would be proud.

Headmaster Coen has informed us that Dominants from all over the world will be attending the ceremony tonight. For those of us interested, we can offer our collar to the Dom of our choice after the graduation ceremony has ended.

I get giddy thinking about it, because we get three

private interviews with prospective Doms to determine whom we feel is our perfect match. We submissives get to decide!

However, there's always the chance the Dominant we choose will decline the offer, like what happened to Brie Bennett at her Collaring Ceremony.

The thing I admire most about Brie is the courage it took for her to put her heart on the line like that—and look at her now. She's a famous film director, collared to the man of her dreams.

And I want to be just like Brie.

I have ever since we met on the commuter train when she handed me the business card that literally changed the course of my life.

In preparation for the evening, I spend the afternoon primping myself as if I am preparing for my own wedding. Because a formal Collaring Ceremony is a lot like that. It's done in front of the BDSM community, so everyone can share in the moment. Wearing a collar is a physical representation of your commitment to your Dominant—and his commitment to you.

It's a beautiful thing.

After spending the afternoon at the hair stylist and getting a manicure and a pedicure, I put on the outfit I have chosen for the big occasion.

I tighten the laces of the amethyst corset that not only complements my blonde hair, but also gives my small breasts a nice boost. I then slip on a flirty ruffled skirt that shows off my bare legs. I'm choosing not to wear garters and hose tonight because the sexy purple pumps contrast well with my naked skin.

For jewelry, I put on only one item, the jeweled cat ears that Captain gave me. I glance at the mirror, pleased with my look. It's flirtatious and fun.

The only thing missing is a pretty collar around my neck…

Headmaster Coen gathers us for a last-minute talk.

"Tonight, we will begin with the Graduation Ceremony. Afterward, you will spend your evening socializing with the D/s community at large. Feel free to speak with whomever you wish. Everyone here has come to celebrate your accomplishment. Then, at the allotted time, you will begin your interviews with the Dominants."

I smile at my other classmates, wondering how many of us will be offering our collars before the night is through.

Master Anderson has been assigned to watch over me during the night's events. I'm excited to be paired with the sexy Dom, especially after finding out he has quite the sense of humor, once you get to know him.

I have worked hard these last six weeks and, in the process, I have become comfortable in who I am and what my future holds.

Feeling a surge of deep pride, I walk up to the stage when I hear my name called. I am amazed at how they've transformed the commons with gold and black tapestries lining the walls—the place now looks regal and elegant.

I stand beside Headmaster Coen, proud of my

achievement. I've discovered strengths I never knew existed and, through the challenges presented in the school's curriculum, I have harnessed an inner power that has made me stronger as a person.

Headmaster Coen tells the assembly, "Of all the students here, Miss Cox has shown the most growth and is being presented with the Pursuit of Excellence Award."

I look at him in surprise, never expecting such an honor. The commons erupts in applause, but the only person I notice in the large crowd is Captain.

He smiles and nods at me.

After the applause dies down, Headmaster Coen turns to me and gives me a handshake. "Congratulations, Miss Cox. Job well done."

"Thank you, Headmaster."

I walk over to Mr. Gallant next, and he hands me the award. "You make us all proud, Miss Cox."

I tear up when I confess, "I've heard through the grapevine that you were my scholarship sponsor. I don't know how I can ever thank you."

The distinguished Dom's cheeks actually blush. "I can say with all honesty that seeing your growth has been a true gift and eclipses anything I may have contributed."

Hearing the next graduate's name called, I leave the stage and Master Anderson holds out his arm to me, stating, "Tonight is the time to be selfish, Miss Cox. You need to be discerning about whom you spend your time with. I suggest you concentrate on those you are most interested in interviewing."

"That is sound advice," I reply, grateful for his insight.

He smiles down at me. "With that in mind, if you need me to steer anyone away, just snap your fingers and I'll be on them like a bee to honey."

"But I would hate to be so rude," I protest.

"Not rude at all," he assures me. "All the Dominants understand the protocol for this evening. As you can see, there is a dance floor, should you wish to utilize it tonight with any of the Dominants. I have only one stipulation—the last dance is mine."

Master Anderson winks at me as he leaves so I can freely mingle on my own.

I don't see Captain, but Brie and Sir Davis are near-by, so I make my way over to them. As soon as Brie sees me approach, her whole face lights up. "Oh Candy, what an exciting night this is for you!"

I give Brie a hug before turning to Sir Davis. "Thank you both for coming."

He smiles. "Congratulations, Miss Cox. I know how rigorous the curriculum is. You should be proud of your exceptional achievements."

I totally blush. Whenever Sir Davis addresses me, I get a little weak in the knees. His dominance is both irresistible and powerful and since he is the former Headmaster of the school, I don't want to do anything that might embarrass myself.

Brie asks excitedly, "Are you ready for your inter-views?"

"I am. I can't wait, really. Thanks so much for shar-ing your questions. I found them very helpful when creating my own."

"It's important," Brie assures me. "You'll learn

things about each Dom that may change your opinion of your compatibility with them."

"Clarity is what I'm hoping for, although I'm certain who it is," I confess.

"I advise you to keep an open mind," Sir Davis reminds me, glancing at Brie with a subtle smirk.

Brie smiles at him, then leans forward to whisper in my ear, "Trust your instincts."

I give her a nod as I catch a glance of Captain in the crowd. "Oh, I hope you two will excuse me."

"Of course, Miss Cox," Sir Davis replies. "Make the most of your evening."

I bow my head in respect. "I certainly will, Sir Davis."

I make a beeline for Captain.

"I'm glad to see you, Captain," I tell him, trying to sound sophisticated and calm even though my heart is racing and I am giddy with excitement.

"Miss Cox, I've only come to observe the graduation." He continues, looking slightly uncomfortable, "I hold a special fondness for you and am pleased to see this day has come."

"Your praise means the world to me," I admit with a flirtatious smile. I hope to tell him so much more during our interview. He doesn't know how I really feel.

He nods curtly. "Just an honest opinion. Don't let me keep you." Captain moves on to talk with Mr. Gallant on the other side of the room, leaving me standing by myself.

Master Anderson is instantly by my side as I watch Captain walk away. "The night is still young. Make me proud by circulating, Miss Cox." His easy cowboy charm calms my nerves.

I seek out Baron next. His smile as I approach warms my heart.

"Look at you now," he states with pride. "You brighten up this whole place." He takes my hand and spins me around slowly like a ballerina, stating, "The difference is like night and day."

I look up into his hazel eyes. The fact is, the allure of Baron's dominance is irresistible, but there's an easiness about him that makes me feel secure.

"Would you like to dance, Miss Cox?" he asks when the music starts.

"Please."

I look to Master Anderson, who gives me a thumbs-up, and I grin as we head onto the dance floor. I'm so tiny, and Baron is so tall, that my eyes are level with his muscular torso. Despite our size difference, he guides me effortlessly in his arms as we dance.

"I will be forever grateful to you for taking care of Liege, Baron."

"I'm not the only one who had a hand in it, but I'm glad to see you're not only adjusted, but thriving."

"Everyone on the staff has been kind and thoughtful, and my weekly sessions with Dr. Reinstrum are really helping me to work things through."

"The staff here is the finest," Baron states proudly. "They go above and beyond to ensure the success of their students. It's an honor for me to work with them."

I've already decided to interview Baron tonight. Although we never had the chance to scene together during my training, I had the privilege of watching him with several of my classmates. I know we don't share the same kink, but he would be a healthy challenge for me, and his level of care is inspiring.

After our dance, I break off and seek out Dominare, the fair-haired Spanish Dom who was paired with me the second night of class because he matched the preferences I'd listed on my application. The trainers hit the nail on the head as far as my physical attraction to him. However, I'm curious to find out how well matched we are outside of a scene.

When the time comes for my first interview, Master Anderson escorts me to a private room and asks for my first interviewee.

"Captain," I state confidently.

He raises an eyebrow, but nods. "As you wish, Miss Cox."

I sit down on the leather couch, waiting anxiously for his return. I know Captain is concerned about our age difference, but I don't care. We are good for each other and I adore everything about him. The basis of all healthy D/s relationships begins with a submissive who is devoted to her Master, and a Dominant who is committed to his sub's care. The two of us meet that requirement, *and* we share the same kink. More than that, I deeply admire Captain. I can't think of anyone I would rather be collared to.

I know he is reluctant to collar me because of my age, but I'm determined to convince him otherwise tonight.

I lower myself to the floor and bow my head, my

heart beating rapidly as I wait for him to enter the room.

"It took a little persuasion, but I got your man here," Master Anderson says with an imaginary tip of a hat before closing the door.

"Miss Cox."

His voice sends pleasant chills through me, and I lift my head, looking at Captain in adoration.

He sighs, pushing his hair back, with a look of exasperation on his face.

I stand up and smile, undaunted. "Thank you for coming. There's something I need to tell you."

Captain stares at me, a look of pain in his eyes. "I shouldn't be here. You shouldn't waste another second on me, Candy."

It's the first time he has called me by my given name, and it brings tears to my eyes. "You're the only one I want. I'm required to choose three to interview, but it has only ever been you."

He shakes his head. "Please don't say that."

"Why?"

"I'm too old…and broken."

"But you're not. You're everything I need." Tears well up in my eyes when I tell him the secret I've been holding inside. "Captain, I lo—"

"Don't say it. I beg you."

"Why?"

He closes his eyes, his brow furrowed in pain. "I'm not the man for you, no matter how much I wish it was otherwise."

I rush to him. "But you are, Captain. You're kind and honorable. We even share the same passions. There's no one better suited to me."

Captain opens his eyes with a look of resignation.

With slow movements, he takes off his eye patch and looks at me. "I'm thirty-six years older than you and I'm defective. As a man of good conscience, I could never collar you."

My bottom lip begins to tremble. "I don't care about your age. I love everything about you, including your scars."

He shakes his head. "You're only thinking about this moment. You have a bright future ahead. I can't be a part of that, don't you see?"

"No. I don't see that at all."

"That's your youthful enthusiasm talking. Trust me, it wouldn't take long to regret such a commitment. I want to spare you that." He grazes my cheek in his thumb. "All I want is for you to have a long and carefree life. That's it."

He looks at me tenderly. "It may be selfish on my part, but I want you to have all the things I missed. You won't have them with me…"

I shake my head, smiling up at him. "Captain, I'm not some silly girl. I'm much older than my years. I have loved and lost, and suffered deeply for my mistakes. The life you see ahead for me is not the life I want. I want stability. I want kindness, and gentle guidance. All those things I find in you."

"Please, you're making this so much harder than it has to be…" He looks at me with a hint of regret.

But I will not be deterred.

I undress and stand before him. "Look at me, Captain. Please."

After a moment, his gaze finally meets mine.

"Answer me truthfully. If we were the same age, would you hesitate?"

"No," he answers in a gruff voice.

"Then let's embrace this rare gift we've been given. Love has no limits."

I can tell my words are having an effect on him when his pained expression softens.

Taking it as an invitation, I stand on tiptoe to give him a gentle but lingering kiss. His low groan causes butterflies in my stomach.

Captain opens his eyes and looks at me longingly—in that moment, I see the confident, virile man he was at eighteen.

He pulls me to him, kissing me hard, releasing the passion he's denied himself for so long. I receive it, begging for more. Captain lifts me up, grasping my thighs in his strong grip as he pushes me against a wall.

I am swept away, blinded by the ferocity of our need for each other.

Without warning, I hear the final bell, having somehow missed the initial one marking ten minutes before the end of our interview.

I look at Captain desperately. "I'm not ready."

He kisses me on the forehead and sets me down gently.

There's a knock on the door. "Miss Cox, it's time for your next interview."

Captain puts on his eye patch and adjusts his erection before facing the door. He looks back at me, our need for each other unquenched.

Master Anderson knocks again.

"Don't worry, Master Anderson. We're finished…for now." I smile at Captain confidently.

Captain leans down and gives me one last, drawn-out kiss before heading out the door.

"Did you get through all your questions?" Master Anderson asks after he leaves.

I laugh to myself. I didn't ask a single one of them. However, I tell him confidently, "I got all the answers I need."

"Good. Who should I call next?"

"Baron, please."

"Your wish is my command."

I pace while I wait for Baron. All those feelings Captain has stirred are swirling inside me. I touch my lips, remembering his last kiss. I can't wait to follow it up tonight—wearing his collar.

Baron strides into the room with a sexy smirk on his lips and says in his low baritone, "You called…"

I walk to the couch and pat the area beside me. "I have a few questions for you, Baron."

He sits down. "Before we begin, I insist on a kiss."

I grin and nod my consent.

Baron leans down and presses his full lips against mine. I moan softly as his tongue enters my mouth and we taste each other for the first time. My heart races. There's no denying there's chemistry between us.

When he pulls back, he growls seductively. "I suspected you'd taste sweet."

I blush. "I *am* Candy."

He chuckles. "I may need another taste."

"First the questions," I insist. "I didn't get very far with my first."

"May I ask who it was?"

"Captain."

Baron nods his head. "A fine gentleman."

"Agreed, but this interview is about you."

He sits back in a relaxed manner. "Bring it on, Miss Cox."

"First question. How long have you been a Dominant?"

"Seven years."

I appreciate his many years of experience, and follow it up with, "So what got you started?"

"I met a girl who was into kink. One thing led to another. I went on to embrace the lifestyle while she went on to other men."

"Ah, that's so sad."

"Not at all. Turned out we weren't compatible."

I laugh lightly, enjoying how easy it is to talk with him. "I know this may seem like an odd question, but what kind of a relationship do you have with your mother?"

"I love my mom. She's got more energy than you and I put together," Baron says with a chuckle. "She's always finding new charities and projects to get involved in. She believes in community and does everything she can to help."

My heart melts, watching Baron's face as he talks about his mother. There's so much pride and love in his voice. I have little doubt that Baron would make a great partner, but my heart belongs to Captain.

So I decide to be upfront with him. "Baron, I think you are an amazing person, but I need to confess something."

He leans forward, a knowing smile on his lips. "Don't tell me."

"What do you think I'm going to say?"

He chuckles. "I could tell it by your kiss. It was the reason I insisted. You have already bound your heart to another."

I look at him sadly. "I hope I haven't upset you."

"Not at all. I know you're required to choose three, and I consider myself lucky to be one of them. It's nice to finally spend time with you." He adds with a smirk, "The kiss was an added bonus."

I blush. "You are a talented kisser."

"If you ever have need of these lips, you let me know."

The ten-minute warning bell rings.

"Why don't I escort you out, Miss Cox? We can spend the last few minutes on the dance floor."

"That is the perfect way to end it."

As we walk out of the interview early, I see the surprised look on Master Anderson's face. I give him a thumbs-up and head out to the dance floor with Baron.

As we move around the floor, I keep hoping to catch a glimpse of Captain. After the song ends, Baron leads me over to Master Anderson.

"Are you satisfied, Miss Cox?" he asks after Baron walks away to speak with Brie.

"Baron is every bit the gentleman I expected he'd

be," I answer.

"And your final choice?"

"Actually, before I say, can you tell me if you've seen Captain? I couldn't spot him while I was dancing."

"He left, Miss Cox."

I look at Master Anderson in shock. "You must be mistaken."

He shakes his head. "I'm sorry."

Without even thinking, I bolt. I don't bother heading to the elevator, taking the stairs instead. I race out into the night, searching for Captain's green vehicle in the parking lot, but it's not there.

Gone.

I wander to the end of the parking lot in a daze and sit down on a concrete block. I know why he left.

He left for me…

Captain admitted he feels the same. I felt it when we kissed so passionately that we lost all sense of the world.

He left because of that need to protect me, convinced that our age difference impedes our happiness— but it doesn't. He doesn't realize how much I need him in my life, and it is up to me to prove it to him.

I see the dark form of Master Anderson's impressive frame walking toward me. "Are you okay, darlin'?"

I stand up and answer, "I will be."

"Good. Although I must point out that you are late for your last interview."

I stare at the ground. "I'm sorry, Master Anderson. I have no wish to interview anyone else."

"Considering the circumstances, I understand. However, I insist you return to the festivities, because you still owe me a dance." He guides me back into the Center, and I feel the stares of everyone on me while he leads me to the center of the room and we begin dancing.

I glance around nervously, making missteps as we go.

"It doesn't matter what anyone thinks," he says calmly. "This is your moment to shine. You've earned this celebration, Miss Cox. Embrace your achievement so you can look back on it in the years to come. The rest will fall into place as it should."

I look up at him, knowing he's right. "Thank you, Master Anderson."

He winks at me. "I knew, even though you're an itty-bitty thing, you had the heart of a lion."

Loving Her

Captain

After returning home from Candy's graduation ceremony, I feel profoundly unsettled. I turn on the TV for noise, attempting to drown out my warring emotions.

On an intellectual level, I know I have done the right thing. However, I have never felt such disquiet in my soul.

I curse fate that I wasn't born twenty years later. Candy is the elusive element I've been missing in my life. To be handed the very thing I want most, but to be forced to walk away from it...

I sit on the couch, patting myself on the back for being man enough to leave her, but it is ripping me to shreds inside.

I turn off the TV and head to bed, needing the escape of sleep. But in the dark, I am haunted by the fear that I have made the biggest mistake of my life.

The feeling only intensifies when I wake up the next

morning. I cannot control the anxiety, so I dress in sweats for a long run, determined to get it out of my system.

As I tie my sneakers, I hear the doorbell ring and open the door to find Candy standing there.

"Good morning, Captain."

"What are you doing here?"

"I wanted to finish what we started last night."

I frown. Does she not understand how hard this is on me? "There is nothing left to discuss," I answer curtly.

Her eyes soften in response to my harsh voice. "Captain, may I come in?"

I shouldn't, but I cannot resist those big doe eyes and step aside, letting her pass. I direct her to the couch, uncertain of her agenda.

"Miss Cox…"

She shakes her head, smiling. "It's Candy to you."

She's so incredibly charming, despite how things ended last night. It's disconcerting. I would have expected tears and accusations thrown my way.

"Why are you here, Miss Cox?"

When Candy meets my gaze, I'm captivated. Her gentle presence is already having a calming effect on me.

"I know why you left last night, Captain. It makes me more certain about my feelings toward you. Only an honorable man would do such a thing."

"I left you."

"Because you love me."

I shake my head.

She just smiles and leans forward, giving me a gentle

kiss on the lips.

That simple kiss unravels me—nothing could keep me from kissing her back. The passionate feelings from the night before ignites as I grasp the back of her neck and kiss her more deeply. Candy melts into my embrace, her lips soft and supple. When she makes a mewing sound, I am completely undone.

"I need you, Captain."

Her words chip away at the last of my resolve, but I gather my senses and fight against it. "We shouldn't. You should go."

Candy's smile widens. She is unlike any other woman I've ever known. Her sureness in the face of my outward opposition is inspiring.

"Let's finish what we started," she murmurs alluringly, looking down at the floor as she waits for my answer.

She has left it up to me to decide, but she must know what that kiss has done to me. I'm unable to walk away from her now.

"Let's."

Candy gazes up, her eyes luminous with desire. I kiss her again, lifting her up in my arms and carrying her to my bedroom. Although I have a great need for her, I undress her slowly, wanting to make love to her body, rather than just claim it.

"Oh, Captain," she moans as I settle between her legs and begin licking and teasing her clit. Everything about her body is alluring. Her tiny frame, her taste, those perky nipples, and that playful smile. I feel as if she was specially designed for me as I explore her body—kissing, licking, and teasing her with my mouth.

Soon, however, she begs me to take her. After last night's encounter, I have no power to resist those wishes. I reach over to my nightstand for a condom.

"Let me," she says, taking the package from me. With a seductive smile, she rips it open with her teeth. I take satisfaction in watching her slowly slip the rubber sheath down over my cock.

I hold her tiny body in my arms and kiss her deeply as I push my cock against her wet opening. There is no full and sudden thrust.

No, I make slow, passionate love to this extraordinary woman.

She stares up at me with a look I haven't seen before—the feeling it evokes is so strong tears well up in my eye. I have never been so affected.

Rather than using my cock for our mutual pleasure, I bond with Candy in a way I have never bonded with another soul.

Afterward, Candy lays her head on my chest, making a purring sound. "I never knew I could feel this way again."

"What do you mean?"

"I feel safe and cherished like I did with Ethan."

I smile, grateful I can provide her that comfort. "I'm glad your first love showered you with the love and care you deserve."

She looks up at me. "What was your first love like, Captain?"

"It didn't end well, but it was sweet while it lasted."

"What happened?" Candy asks, sounding concerned.

I shrug, keeping my answer short. "Dear John

letter."

"No!" she protests. "That's so heartless."

I stroke her soft hair. There was a time when those memories hurt, but I've been through too much since to feel any pain about it now. "I only hope she found what she was looking for."

"You are far kinder than I am," Candy confesses.

"Not so. I'm just a lot older, and age tends to give a person a different perspective."

Candy lays her head back down on my chest, sighing contentedly. "I love you."

The minute the words escape her lips, I feel a twisting in my gut. Not because I don't feel the same way, but because I cannot voice those feelings to her.

I know if I were to make that mistake, Candy would grab on to it, sacrificing her future for me. I cannot let her do that. I smile down at Candy, continuing to stroke her hair as I imagine her as a mother and, much later, playing with her grandchildren.

That is her future—not mine.

She runs her fingers over my arm in a gentle caress, then turns my hand to stare at my wrist. Curious, she takes a closer look. "All this time, I thought this was some kind of birthmark." She smiles up at me. "But it's a cluster of grapes."

I look at the tattoo on my wrist and feel a stab of pain. I take a moment before replying. "It's in honor of a buddy."

Candy caresses the area with her finger. "He must have been important to you."

"He and I went through a lot together," I answer in a

strained voice.

"What was his name?"

I pull my hand away. "No."

Candy looks at me with compassion. "It's okay. I understand if you don't want to talk. You're safe with me."

Her last words echo in my head as we lie there in silence. Finally, I share, "A part of me died that day."

She nods. "I felt like I died the day Ethan was killed."

"In some ways…we did. You and I became different people because of the losses we've suffered."

"It's one of the reasons we fit together so perfectly." She takes my hand and kisses it. "You're my safe haven."

Candy is dangerous. She makes it far too easy to forget the barriers that separate us.

We lie there in silence, comforted by each other's presence.

"Captain…?"

"Yes."

"I know you're convinced that if we were born at different times, it would make a difference. But you're wrong. We're perfect for each other right now—just as we are."

"But why would you want an ugly cuss like me?"

Candy laughs softly, caressing my scarred cheek. "I love this face. There's nothing ugly about it."

She kisses me softly on the lips.

Damn, she makes resisting her impossible.

"I am not looking for forever, Captain. I just want your love now."

I have thought of nothing else but Candy and our conversation.

I hear the sound of her voice and smell her sweet scent at odd times when I am alone during the day. It's as if we are already connected, and it seems foolish to keep her at a distance when we both know what we want.

After finally making the decision, I head to a jewelry designer I met through Celestia, Marquis Gray's submissive.

The jewelry designer sits me down and asks me to explain the piece I want made.

"It is an unusual request," I warn him.

"Not an issue," he assures me. "We have many clients from the BDSM community."

"Excellent. Then I would like you to make a delicate patent leather collar studded with diamonds and a gold heart locket engraved with this message on the front and back." I slip a piece of paper with the details to him.

Looking at the paper, he replies with a smile, "This must be a very cherished pet. Is this a Christmas gift?"

"No, it is not."

He nods and asks, "What color for the collar?"

"Pink. I'll also need a gold chain leash with a black leather handle."

"Not pink to match the collar?"

I chuckle. "The collar is for her to wear. The leash is for me to use—so, no pink."

"Fair enough. I should be able to have this ready within three weeks."

I leave the jewelry shop feeling the exuberance of a young kid of eighteen. Candy has changed my entire outlook on life. I've spent years living in my head, tormented by those I could not save.

It served no purpose—even then, I knew it.

However, it wasn't until Candy burst into my life that I could see a new path and was able to focus on my life. I am not blind to the insurmountable barrier of time that stands between us. A force that cannot be altered. We are two people born out of sync by thirty-six years, but Candy only sees us and I am beginning to, as well.

I accept that this is temporary. There will come a time when I will have to set her free to live her life. Even though it will hurt like hell to let her go, I will do so with a full heart.

Candy…

Just her name brings a smile to my lips, and I am a man not used to smiling.

Candy claims I am her safe haven but, in truth, she is mine.

I've dressed in my formal military uniform for the occasion. I tuck the box with her collar inside my suit jacket before I button up and look at the mirror. It has been a long time since I've donned this uniform.

It carries with it both pride for my country and sorrow for those lost under my command. Today, however, I will add a new memory—the intimacy of a private collaring ceremony—for just the two of us.

I feel anxious on the drive there, and doubly so as I walk up to her apartment door. Even though this is something we both desire, I hesitate for a second before knocking.

I stand back and clasp my hands behind my back as I wait.

A woman in her forties answers the door. I can see hints of Candy's features in her face and suspect this must be her mother.

"Oh, wow…" she replies, her gaze darting up to my injured face and settling on my eyepatch. She quickly looks away and blushes. "Are you here for a donation?"

I smile awkwardly, unsure how to respond.

The door opens wider and I'm met by a man who must be Candy's father, also significantly younger than I.

"We already gave, but we're always willing to help out Toys for Tots." He reaches into his pants and whips out his wallet, handing me several bills.

He's confused me for a Marine, so I explain as I try to give the money back to him, "No. That's not why I'm here."

He holds up his hands. "Don't worry about it. Whatever charity you represent, we support you and the military one hundred percent. Thank you for your service."

His wife echoes, "Yes, thank you for your service." I can tell she finds my face disturbing because she can't bear to look at me now.

"I don't want to appear rude, but we're surprising our daughter. She doesn't know we've come to celebrate the holidays with her," Candy's father explains, looking at his watch. "She's due any minute."

My gut lurches and tightens as I stare at Candy's parents, facing the cold reality of our age difference. I was mistaken to think that collaring their young daughter was the right thing to do. I've been deluding myself...

"I will be on my way then," I mumble, nodding to them both.

"Merry Christmas," Mrs. Cox calls out before quickly shutting the door.

I rush out of the building, not wanting Candy to see me here. As I pass by a bell ringer for the Salvation Army, I quickly stuff the cash her father gave me into the slot of the red pot.

"Thank you, sir, and happy holidays!" the old woman calls out cheerily as I hurry on.

I berate myself for being such a fool.

Candy has her whole life ahead of her. It's not right to complicate it with a relationship that's doomed from the start.

I get back into my vehicle and speed off, but not before I see Candy stopped at the light in front of me, both of us waiting on opposite sides of the street for it to change. She's bouncing in her seat, moving to the beat of an old Christmas song blasting from her car.

I choke up, seeing how youthful and carefree she is when she thinks no one is watching.

I don't want to be the one to quell that carefree spirit. I can't do that to her.

I love Candy—therefore, I must let her go.

As the light turns green, we start toward each other. She's oblivious to me, belting out the lyrics of the song on the radio.

I look at Candy one last time as we pass.

Goodbye, my pet.

I hope you enjoyed **Safe Haven!**

Coming next is—**Destined to Dominate**, the conclusion of Captain's Duet.
Click here to read the next book!

Love has no boundaries…
Candy is not about to let Captain go.
Find out what happens when true love collides with selfless sacrifice.
Sparks are about to fly in the heartfelt conclusion
to Captain and Candy's story.
~Red
(Release Date – August 21, 2018)

Or, if you are new to Brie and the gang, you can begin the journey with the 1st Box Set of
Brie's Submission which is FREE!

COMING NEXT

Destined to Dominate (Captain's Duet) the 2nd book of Captain's story

Available for Preorder

Reviews mean the world to me!

I truly appreciate you taking the time to review *Safe Haven*.

If you could leave a review on both Goodreads and the site where you purchased this eBook from, I would be so grateful. Sincerely, ~Red

Don't miss the background stories behind the characters you read about in *Safe Haven.*

You can begin the journey with the 1ˢᵗ Box Set of *Brie's Submission* which is FREE!

ABOUT THE AUTHOR

Over Two Million readers have enjoyed Red's stories

Red Phoenix – USA Today Bestselling Author
Winner of 8 Readers' Choice Awards

Hey Everyone!

I'm Red Phoenix, an author who also happens to be a submissive in real life. I wrote the Brie's Submission series because I wanted people everywhere to know just how much fun BDSM can be.

There is a huge cast of characters who are part of Brie's journey. The further you read into the story the more you learn about each one. I hope you grow to love Brie and the gang as much as I do.

They've become like family.

When I'm not writing, you can find me online with readers.

I heart my fans! ~Red

To find out more visit my Website

redphoenixauthor.com

Follow Me on BookBub

bookbub.com/authors/red-phoenix

Newsletter: Sign up

redphoenixauthor.com/newsletter-signup

Facebook: RedPhoenix69

Twitter: @redphoenix69

Instagram: RedPhoenixAuthor

I invite you to join my reader Group!

facebook.com/groups/539875076052037

SIGN UP FOR MY NEWSLETTER
HERE FOR THE LATEST RED
PHOENIX UPDATES

SALES, GIVEAWAYS, NEW
RELEASES, EXCLUSIVE SNEAK
PEEKS, AND MORE!
SIGN UP HERE
REDPHOENIXAUTHOR.COM/NEWSLETTER-
SIGNUP

Red Phoenix is the author of:

Brie's Submission Series:
Teach Me #1
Love Me #2
Catch Me #3
Try Me #4
Protect Me #5
Hold Me #6
Surprise Me #7
Trust Me #8
Claim Me #9
Enchant Me #10
A Cowboy's Heart #11
Breathe with Me #12
Her Russian Knight #13
Under His Protection #14
Her Russian Returns #15
In Sir's Arms #16
Bound by Love #17

*You can also purchase the AUDIO BOOK **Versions**

Also part of the Submissive Training Center world:

Captain's Duet
Safe Haven
Destined to Dominate

Other Books by Red Phoenix

Blissfully Undone
* Available in eBook and paperback

(Snowy Fun—Two people find themselves snowbound in a cabin where hidden love can flourish, taking one couple on a sensual journey into ménage à trois)

His Scottish Pet: Dom of the Ages
* Available in eBook and paperback

Audio Book: *His Scottish Pet: Dom of the Ages*

(Scottish Dom—A sexy Dom escapes to Scotland in the late 1400s. He encounters a waif who has the potential to free him from his tragic curse)

The Erotic Love Story of Amy and Troy
* Available in eBook and paperback

(Sexual Adventures—True love reigns, but fate continually throws Troy and Amy into the arms of others)

eBooks

Varick: The Reckoning

(Savory Vampire—A dark, sexy vampire story. The hero navigates the dangerous world he has been thrust into with lusty passion and a pure heart)

———————————

Keeper of the Wolf Clan (Keeper of Wolves, #1)

(Sexual Secrets—A virginal werewolf must act as the clan's mysterious Keeper)

———————————

The Keeper Finds Her Mate (Keeper of Wolves, #2)

(Second Chances—A young she-wolf must choose between old ties or new beginnings)

———————————

The Keeper Unites the Alphas (Keeper of Wolves, #3)

(Serious Consequences—The young she-wolf is captured by the rival clan)

———————————

Boxed Set: Keeper of Wolves Series (Books 1-3)

(Surprising Secrets—A secret so shocking it will rock Layla's world. The young she-wolf is put in a position of being able to save her werewolf clan or becoming the reason for its destruction)

Socrates Inspires Cherry to Blossom

(Satisfying Surrender—A mature and curvaceous woman becomes fascinated by an online Dom who has much to teach her)

By the Light of the Scottish Moon

(Saving Love—Two lost souls, the Moon, a werewolf, and a death wish…)

In 9 Days

(Sweet Romance—A young girl falls in love with the new student, nicknamed "the Freak")

9 Days and Counting

(Sacrificial Love—The sequel to *In 9 Days* delves into the emotional reunion of two longtime lovers)

And Then He Saved Me

(Saving Tenderness—When a young girl tries to kill herself, a man of great character intervenes with a love that heals)

Play With Me at Noon

(Seeking Fulfillment—A desperate wife lives out her
fantasies by taking five different men in five days)

Connect with Red on Substance B

Substance B is a platform for independent authors to directly connect with their readers. Please visit Red's Substance B page where you can:

- Sign up for Red's newsletter
- Send a message to Red
- See all platforms where Red's books are sold

Visit Substance B today to learn more about your favorite independent authors.